OXFORD

THE COMPL

CHARLES PERRAULT was born in 1628, into a talented family living in Paris. Although he gained legal qualifications his main role was to act as adviser on cultural matters in the royal court. In 1665 he became an aide to Colbert, finance minister to Louis XIV, first on royal buildings and then on the arts and literature generally. Later he was a reforming director of the French Academy. He wrote much, in both prose and verse, and vigorously defended the modernist position in literary controversy. From 1691 he wrote a series of verse and prose *contes*, or tales, and in 1697 published the *Histoires ou Contes du temps passé, avec des moralités*, the fairy tales for which he is best known. Perrault died in 1703.

CHRISTOPHER BETTS was senior lecturer in French Studies at the University of Warwick until his retirement. He is the author of academic studies and translator of Montesquieu's *Persian Letters* (Penguin) and Rousseau's *Social Contract* (Oxford World's Classics).

*Reading the tales to the family*

OXFORD WORLD'S CLASSICS

CHARLES PERRAULT

# The Complete Fairy Tales

*Translated with an Introduction and Notes by*
CHRISTOPHER BETTS

OXFORD
UNIVERSITY PRESS

# OXFORD

UNIVERSITY PRESS

Great Clarendon Street, Oxford OX2 6DP

Oxford University Press is a department of the University of Oxford.
It furthers the University's objective of excellence in research, scholarship,
and education by publishing worldwide in

Oxford New York

Auckland Cape Town Dar es Salaam Hong Kong Karachi
Kuala Lumpur Madrid Melbourne Mexico City Nairobi
New Delhi Shanghai Taipei Toronto

With offices in

Argentina Austria Brazil Chile Czech Republic France Greece
Guatemala Hungary Italy Japan Poland Portugal Singapore
South Korea Switzerland Thailand Turkey Ukraine Vietnam

Oxford is a registered trade mark of Oxford University Press
in the UK and in certain other countries

Published in the United States
by Oxford University Press Inc., New York

© Christopher Betts 2009

The moral rights of the author have been asserted
Database right Oxford University Press (maker)

First published 2009

First published as an Oxford World's Classics paperback 2010

All rights reserved. No part of this publication may be reproduced,
stored in a retrieval system, or transmitted, in any form or by any means,
without the prior permission in writing of Oxford University Press,
or as expressly permitted by law, or under terms agreed with the appropriate
reprographics rights organization. Enquiries concerning reproduction
outside the scope of the above should be sent to the Rights Department,
Oxford University Press, at the address above

You must not circulate this book in any other binding or cover
and you must impose the same condition on any acquirer

British Library Cataloguing in Publication Data

Data available

Library of Congress Cataloging-in-Publication Data

Data available

Typeset by Glyph International, Bangalore, India
Printed in Great Britain by
Clays Ltd, Elcograf S.p.A.

ISBN 978–0–19–958580–9

16

# CONTENTS

❧❧

# LIST OF ILLUSTRATIONS

# INTRODUCTION

❦

Given the title of this volume, the reader will no doubt take for granted that the stories it contains were created by a specific person, by the name of Charles Perrault, writing at a specific time and place—the end of the seventeenth century in Paris. Authorship and historical origins seem guaranteed. But if you look at a collection of stories centred, not on Perrault, but on the tale, say, of Red Riding-Hood,[1] these assumptions may seem shaky. You will find that his *Le Petit Chaperon Rouge* is there regarded as an item of folk literature, one among a huge array of versions of 'the same' tale, collected from many different times and places, without known origins and in most cases without an author. So Perrault did not create the story, he merely gave us one more version, albeit an important one. And seen in another perspective, that of adults recalling their childhood, this volume contains tales that many of us have known and loved for decades, concerning ourselves with meaning sufficiently in order to enjoy the narrative, as the child does, and no more; but if you look again at what you may remember as pleasurable entertainment, you will find that the content of the tales is problematic, to put it mildly. They are full of savagery, deceit, and sexual implications which are more or less evident—very much so in the most notorious verse tale, *Donkey-Skin*. It is understandable that readers ask what such stories signify, both for child and adult.

Assuming for the moment that Perrault was indeed responsible for the tales (and leaving till later the long-standing question whether his son Pierre wrote at least some of them), it should also be said that his position as an author is anomalous. He wrote much, on many subjects, but only a few 'fairy-tales', the usual though rather misleading

[1] For example in the relevant section of the basic work on French folk-tale, by Paul Delarue and Marie-Louise Tenèze, continued by Josianne Bru, *Le Conte populaire français*, catalogue raisonné . . ., 5 vols., Paris: various publishers (1957–2000).

term.[2] They have been translated and published all over the world, and in consequence are almost certainly better known than any other French work. Yet in literary history they are largely neglected, and most people who know the tales would not recognize his name. The film that is clearly an amplified version of Perrault's tale is commonly called Walt Disney's *Cinderella*.

These stories raise plenty of problems, then, and an introduction can do no more than indicate some lines of approach. For the literary critic, the *Contes* are admired and studied because Perrault was a master of narrative; the quality of the writing is paramount. But as regards interpretation, the methods of pure literary criticism are insufficient. From psychoanalysis we need to take not only insights into child psychology, but also the post-Freudian interpretation of symbolism. Even more necessary are the data which come from folk-tale studies; comparisons between Perrault's version of a tale and others are of fundamental interest. Some are mentioned here, but Appendix A gives further detail in the form of summaries of tales which throw light in one way or another on the versions handed down to us by Perrault.

## 1. *Perrault and His Works*

Perrault was born in 1628, into a family then undistinguished, but of many talents. He made an extremely successful career under the 'absolute monarchy' of Louis XIV, who in 1661, as a young man, took the reins of government into his own hands. Perrault was the right age to benefit from the King's policy of choosing public servants from commoners rather than the aristocracy. First as an aide to Colbert, Louis's first and greatest minister, a post that Perrault seems to have won by his writing skills, he became responsible for public buildings, and later a leading figure in administering the King's cultural policies. Ousted from his position as 'Contrôleur des bâtiments' when Colbert died, by which time he had made his fortune, he devoted

---

[2] Fairies appear in some but not in others; probably the influence of *Cinderella* has caused the term to be extended to all. Perrault's contemporary Mme d'Aulnoy used the title 'Fairy Tales'.

much energy to the new and still ineffectual Académie française, thus maintaining his influence in the world of official culture. From youth he had been a talented and industrious writer, especially in verse; in tandem with his administrative career, and in a manner which typifies the conjunction between literary and worldly success at the time, he wrote prolifically in praise, direct or indirect, of Louis XIV and his achievements, from the mottos on commemorative medals to panegyrics on military victories. These were not mere attempts to curry favour at court: such writings were an important element in a concerted effort to promote the prestige of the King, seen as personifying the nation. Perrault, then, was a most loyal servant of the crown, and earned rewards in wealth and status. The first Moral of *Puss in Boots* could have been written with himself in mind—he exemplifies the royalist meritocracy which was gradually acquiring power.

By the age of 55 he was effectively in retirement from his career as a public servant, and applied himself to the affairs of the Académie and to writing, producing very varied works, among them several large-scale poems of Christian inspiration. His involvement in the Quarrel of the Ancients and the Moderns, a long-running controversy about the relative merits of contemporary culture as opposed to that of classical antiquity, began when in 1687 he published a poem adroitly associating modernist sentiments with loyalty to the Christian King. The *Siècle de Louis le Grand* ('The Century of Louis the Great') asserted that under Louis the arts had reached heights previously unscaled, thus causing outrage among those who revered the legacy, especially in literature, of the Greek and Roman classics. Their champion was Boileau (1636–1711), the satirist and acknowledged authority on all things literary, who from then on became Perrault's enemy and took every opportunity to mock his work. Perrault followed up the poem with three volumes of a *Parallèle des anciens et des modernes*, his best-known work apart from the *Contes*.

These energetic activities are remote from the world of fairy-tale. Does his personal life explain why, in his sixties, he branched out so unexpectedly from the rewarding paths of public and semi-official poetry? With Perrault, as with virtually all except the grandest figures of the time, very little personal information survives. Apart from a short-lived twin,[3] he was the youngest of seven children, like his character Hop o' my Thumb, except that Perrault's siblings included two sisters. One brother, Claude, became an important architect. The family was close-knit, and the bonds between the siblings of whom anything is known remained strong. Charles soon showed himself to be a strong-minded character, abandoning school on his own initiative at the age of about 15: he walked out, according to his memoirs,[4] having had a row with one of his teachers. Together with a friend, he saw to his own education thereafter, evidently to good effect. His father died in 1653, when Charles was 22; his mother four years later. He married late, in 1672, when he was well able to provide for a wife. She was Marie Guichon, aged only 19. Colbert thought that Perrault should have done better for himself, and offered to find him someone wealthier; this may suggest a love-match.[5] Three sons were born, in 1675, 1676, and 1678, and perhaps a daughter, about whom no details are known;[6] later in 1678, their mother died. Perrault did not remarry. He is known from the testimony of contemporaries to have taken much interest in the upbringing of his children, but it remains unclear whether he himself told them fairy-tales, which was commonly a

---

[3] The first sentence of his *Mémoires de ma vie* (ed. Paul Bonnefon, Paris: Librairie Renouard (1909)), the main source of information, written in 1702, reads: 'I was born on the twelfth of January 1628, one of twins.' The other twin, also a boy, lived only for six months. Marc Soriano, in his *Le Dossier Perrault*, Paris: Hachette (1972), which has much valuable information, bases on this the unsustainable theory that the trauma it caused determined Perrault's psychological development.

[4] *Mémoires*, 111.

[5] This is what Colbert asked (*Mémoires*, 223), probably disapproving of the idea; Perrault relates his answer: that he had seen Marie only once since she had left the convent in which she was educated, but knew her parents well and was certain that he would get on with them. He could have said it merely to placate Colbert.

[6] The birth dates, which are found in baptismal registers, are relevant because, although it is often said that Perrault had four children, there seems to be no record of another birth. That the first record dates from more than three years after the marriage is unusual, though explicable. If there was a birth before 1675, the baptism was apparently not recorded, which, given Perrault's piety, is certainly unusual. The only written record dates from much later, when after the publication of the *Contes* his relative Mlle Lhéritier dedicated one of her stories to 'the sister' of the youngest son, Pierre. Unless this is some private code, the most plausible explanation is a stillborn daughter between 1672 and 1675. Paul Bonnefon, the editor of the *Mémoires*, affirms that only three children were born (223 n. 1).

woman's occupation. However, a passage in the Preface to the *Contes*, in the course of defending the value of his book, mentions that 'fathers and mothers' deserve praise for giving young children early moral instruction by means of such stories.

It was in any case only long afterwards that he began on the course which was to lead towards the prose tales. In 1691 came the first long tale in verse, which is about a wife: *Griselidis*. The subject was taken from one of the great works of European literature, Boccaccio's *Decameron*, of about 1358, in which it is the last story, rather untypical of a work known for comic bawdiness. Its heroine is known in English as Patient Griselda; she is the mistreated wife whose acceptance of her fate finally wins over her cruel husband. Perrault's next tale, also in verse, was a complete contrast: the short and comic *Les Souhaits ridicules*, 'Three Silly Wishes', published in 1693 in the *Mercure galant*, the Parisian literary and social periodical. This was followed by the third and last verse tale, *Donkey-Skin*, also containing a good deal of humour, but on a subject, again taken from folk-tale, which in itself is scarcely comic; the story's opening concerns a widowed father who decides that his daughter must be his second wife. It was published in 1694, but like the two other tales it would certainly have been given private readings beforehand, in one or other of the literary salons; *Griselidis* had been read in a session of the French Academy in 1691.

The salons were regular gatherings, in a drawing-room, of friends and acquaintances of the hostess. They were of enormous significance in the literary and social life of the *ancien régime*. Through the conversations which took place in them, including elaborate intellectual and literary pursuits and pastimes, both men and women could acquire prestige and influence. They seem to have been an important factor in Perrault's move from verse narrative to the prose of the later *Contes*, since a new fashion for fairy-tale originated, it seems, with storytelling in the salons. In 1690 came a story published within a novel by Madame d'Aulnoy,[7] who herself ruled a notable salon. She must have caught something in the public mood, because from then on through

---

[7] 'A lady of good family, good looks, good mind, sharp wit, and strange life (few women can have plotted to have their husband executed for high treason), was the foremost teller of fairy tales in her day, and indeed the innovator, it seems, of the fairy

most of the eighteenth century the fairy-tale genre, or at any rate tales of magic, including oriental tales in the *Arabian Nights*, flourished. The usual explanation is that the dazzling achievements of Louis XIV's early reign were fading into decline, and that in a decade marked also by a series of national disasters (royal deaths, military defeat, spreading poverty, famine) escapist literature was popular.

The majority of the tales published were by women writers, Mme d'Aulnoy foremost among them, and were often entirely invented. When based on traditional tales, they were almost always longer and more obviously literary than Perrault's spare narratives. Some well-known examples were written by a younger relative of his on his mother's side, Mlle Marie-Jeanne Lhéritier (1664–1734),[8] whose salon and writings were to make her in due course a much-respected figure. In Perrault's Preface to his verse tales, he mentions that he sent her a copy—presumably before publication—of *Donkey-Skin*; she responded with her comments. Like him, and at more or less the same time, in 1695, she wrote a version of the tale known in English as 'Diamonds and Toads' (also as 'The Kind and Unkind Sisters'); this was in her *Œuvres mêlées* ('Miscellanies'). The two of them must have discussed their stories but agreed to publish separately. Another case is a tale with the same title as one of Perrault's, *Riquet à la houppe*, by Catherine Bernard, who published it as part of a novel, *Inès de Cordoue*, in 1696; it was probably not simple coincidence that both chose the same subject.

The first of the prose tales appeared in 1695, in manuscript form, not written out by Perrault himself, but by a skilled calligrapher preparing a luxurious presentation volume for a great personage, 'Mademoiselle', that is, the King's niece. She was then 19. The manuscript, entitled *Contes de ma mère l'oie* ('Tales of Mother Goose'), contained five tales, those of Sleeping Beauty, Little Red Riding-Hood,

tale as a literary genre'; Iona and Peter Opie, *The Classic Fairy Tales*, Oxford: Oxford University Press (1974), 24.

[8] She is variously said to be his cousin or his niece. See on her and her work Marina Warner, *From the Beast to the Blonde: On Fairy Tales and Their Tellers*, London: Chatto & Windus (1984), 170–9, who says that her mother and Perrault's were 'either sisters or cousins' (p. 170). Raymonde Robert, in her edition of Mlle Lhéritier's *Contes* (Paris: Champion (2005), 18), argues that she and Perrault were cousins.

Bluebeard, Puss in Boots, and The Fairies. They were introduced by a dedicatory epistle, and from it stems an enduring mystery in Perrault studies, for it is signed 'P.P.'—the initials of Pierre, Charles Perrault's youngest son, also known as Pierre Darmancour, then aged 16 or 17. Were the tales therefore by 'a child', as he is called in the dedication? This and other documentary evidence has often been taken to justify the attribution to Pierre,[9] but evidence from contemporaries in a position to know points the other way. The general points which seem significant are that Pierre gave no other indications of being a writer, and that his father had good reason to conceal his own authorship. It seems reasonable to assume, with the majority, that the attribution to Charles Perrault is correct, if only in the sense that he was responsible for the tales as we have them. It remains possible that Pierre contributed something in the form of an early draft or simply by discussion.

In 1696 a version of *Sleeping Beauty* was published in the *Mercure galant*; it was revised for the complete prose tales. They were published early in 1697, anonymously, and over the imprint of Claude Barbin, the leading publisher of literary works: *Histoires ou Contes du temps passé. Avec des moralités*—'Stories or Tales of Bygone Times. With their Morals'. Three tales were added to those in the manuscript: *Cinderella*, *Ricky the Tuft*, and *Hop o' my Thumb*. The only passages in verse were the 'Moralités', most of which were new in 1697.

Perrault's writings in the closing years of his life were extremely varied, from lives of famous men to a poem on sugar-cane, but the *Contes* were not to have a sequel, despite their immediate popularity. The nearest we find was a work of 1699 translating or adapting some fables by Gabriele Faerno, an Italian writer of the sixteenth century. They imitate La Fontaine in style, with less deftness and grace.[10] Unhappiness centred on Pierre might explain the absence of any further tales: in April 1697, only a few months after the publication of the *Histoires ou Contes*, he had a sword fight with an even younger neighbour, who died as a result. Charles Perrault had to pay a large amount

---

[9] For instance by Soriano, *Le Dossier Perrault*, and elsewhere, and Gérard Gélinas, *Enquête sur les Contes de Perrault*, Paris: Imago (2004).

[10] Gabriele Faerno, *Centum fabulae*, 1564. A selection has been republished by Marc Soriano in his edition of Perrault, Paris: Flammarion (1989).

in compensation. Pierre himself, who became a soldier, died in 1700; his father three years later.

## 2. *The Tales in Verse*

In all sorts of ways, the poem of *Griselda* is an unusual work. It is distinct from the other tales in being (comparatively) realistic: Perrault seems to have believed that the subject was real, for he tried to discover which particular lord of Saluzzo, the northern Italian town in which the action is situated, had married a local girl called Griselda,[11] and the poem's own full title is *La Marquise de Salusses ou la Patience de Griselidis, nouvelle*, the last word indicating a short narrative of a realistic kind, as Perrault observes in the Preface to the tales. Modern readers may disagree, given the stereotyped romantic incidents of a hunt followed by the discovery in a remote spot of a beautiful shepherdess, but a personal drama then unfolds which is certainly an attempt on Perrault's part to portray the more-or-less pathological psychology of the husband and the efforts of his wife to endure her sufferings. She could be described as a secular saint, if not quite a martyr; it may be significant that, among Perrault's other works, the closest in nature to *Griselda* was a long biographical poem, *Saint Paulin*, much derided by Boileau. Christian faith is paramount for Griselda, for whom the marriage oath is absolutely binding; in her worst moments she turns to God, expressing submission to her fate in the style of contemporary devout poetry.

In this respect Perrault revises his source significantly, since in Boccaccio the religious element is unimportant. In England the story was treated by Chaucer, who gives it to the Clerk of Oxford in the *Canterbury Tales*; in France, paradoxically, it was a Latin translation by Petrarch which made it popular, from the late fourteenth century onwards, as a presentation of the highest feminine virtue—helpful for feminist writers defending women against misogynist attacks, of which there were many. It became a staple of the so-called 'biblio thèque bleue', the cheap popular booklets, or chapbooks, in blue

---

[11] See Collinet's edition, Paris: Gallimard (1981), 276.

paper covers, hawked around the country by pedlars. But another great literary figure is important here besides Boccaccio: La Fontaine (1621–95). He had written, besides the famous *Fables*, a notorious collection of verse tales, *Contes* again, of the same genre as those in the *Decameron* and often based on them. Perrault disapproved, despite his admiration for the senior poet, whom he knew. He explains in the Preface that *Griselda* and La Fontaine's tale *La Matrone d'Ephèse* are the same in nature, but criticizes the morality of La Fontaine's poem; the implication, he says, is that there are no truly virtuous women.[12] In sum, Perrault took his subject from Boccaccio, the form from La Fontaine, but rejected the unflattering view of women found frequently in both.

Hostility to women was also, in a particularly vehement style, a feature of Boileau's poetry. Passages in his satires had often attacked them, but in 1694 he published a much longer and more virulent onslaught in his tenth satire. The poem had been long in the making and Perrault had some knowledge of its content well before its publication; among the jumble of intentions from which *Griselda* came we should certainly include the desire to defend women against Perrault's own enemy. He also attacked Boileau in an *Apologie des femmes*, published in a matter of days after the appearance of the tenth satire. It consists of a poem with a long Preface; the defence of women is also a defence of marriage.[13] As to the personal inspiration for the poem, Perrault was a widower devoted, it would seem, to a wife who had died young, and who may or may not have given birth to a daughter. Among the genuinely moving scenes in *Griselda* are some describing the bond between mother and daughter, and the anguish caused by the husband's worst act of cruelty, the removal of the baby from her mother's care; he later tells her that her child has died. It is tempting, though perhaps sentimental, to think that Perrault felt moved to pay tribute to the memory of Marie Guichon, while rebutting the

[12] See below, p. 4. *La Matrone d'Ephèse*, though a 'conte' and not a fable, was published in the last, somewhat miscellaneous twelfth book of the *Fables*, in 1693.

[13] It is in the Preface that Perrault says that he had known about Boileau's satire for some time; he wrote the *Apologie* in advance.

misogynistic views of his old adversary, and chose a well-known model of feminine virtue in order to do so.

Whatever his intentions in writing *Griselda*, its origins should dispel the idea that the poem is hostile to women. Nowadays, to hold up wifely patience for admiration might seem anti-feminist, in that it reinforces the belief that the male is dominant by right; but in the seventeenth century such was the assumption made by virtually every one, not only in Perrault's poem. The law in France, as elsewhere, gave husbands almost unlimited power over their wives, and although contemporaries of feminist views protested, it would have been futile to suggest that, in practice, a wife could do anything but put up with it. Boccaccio's tale had remained popular, it would seem, among women rather than men, because it ends in a triumph, painful but genuine, for the maltreated wife. As in Chaucer, her husband is openly criticized. In Perrault there is an attempt, not entirely convincing, to elucidate his psychology, which looks like an attempt to excuse his admittedly bad behaviour. He is often portrayed in the flattering, but entirely conventional terms invariably used for royalty,[14] but throughout the reader is invited to sympathize with Griselda; several scenes were clearly invented for that purpose.[15]

*Griselda* was from the outset a work of literature. Although its heroine had become, in effect, a figure of folklore, all its antecedents are literary, and no authentic folk-tales are recorded on the subject. The situation is different with Perrault's subsequent stories, verse and prose, which all originate in folk-tale, directly or indirectly.

[14] Collinet (his edition, p. 276), in the course of a résumé of the contribution made by Perrault to the story, notes that the portrait of the Prince is modelled on the young Louis XIV. Since Griselda is something of a Cinderella in advance, the fact that Louis had secretly married the devout Mme de Maintenon, who herself resembled the fairy-tale heroine in more than one respect, suggests the intriguing possibility that Perrault had her in mind when composing his poem. See Antonia Fraser, *Love and Louis XIV*, London: Phoenix (2006), 179–81, on the trials of her childhood, and p. 254 on her view of marriage: 'She must be as submissive towards the King as Sarah was towards Abraham.'

[15] One is the remarkable passage in which she insists that she ought to breast-feed the child herself, in an age when it was usual to employ a wet-nurse. It is Jean-Jacques Rousseau who is always given the credit for first arguing against wet-nurses, in his *Émile* (1761).

The subject of the next, *Three Silly Wishes*, is taken from folk-tale, although showing the influence of salon style in its dedication.[16] Authorities on the subject classify the type of tale in question as religious, because in many versions the wishes are granted by a divine figure, whether Christian or other, but there is no trace of religious feeling in Perrault's tale; Jupiter is the deity inherited from antiquity who had become merely a character in narrative. In *Three Silly Wishes* conjugal relations are the basic subject, as in other versions, which usually poke fun at husband or wife or both. However, the anecdote readily lends itself to more or less obscene treatments, and passing insinuations are frequent.[17] It is possible that Perrault knew of a bawdier version, and cleaned it up to some extent. He could well have been aware of the suggestiveness of the sausage, if the tongue-in-cheek preliminaries are anything to go by; here he makes fun of 'simpering girls' who might be shocked by the subject. If he did in fact make the story less lewd, it would have been consistent with what he had done with a notorious moment in Boccaccio's tale of Griselda: before the marriage, his Marquis has her stripped naked in public, which is said to have been a medieval Tuscan custom.[18] Perrault expunged this detail, though he preserved the scene in which the bride is reclothed. The revision was certainly made consciously, in order to comply with one of the rigid norms of seventeenth-century French writing, *bienséance*, or propriety; with *Three Silly Wishes* we can only guess.

This may be a light-hearted example, but it confirms that, in the matter of origins, all the tales after *Griselda* need to be considered with reference to folk-tale. For present purposes the versions recorded

[16] The tale is again indebted to La Fontaine, many of whose fables are from folk-tale. Like the fabulist, Perrault treats the peasant couple with indulgent mockery, and adds a not-very-serious moral.

[17] The *Arabian Nights* contains an uninhibited version in which the husband wishes, at his wife's behest, for a larger male member, with truly monstrous results. See Ashliman website under Foolish Wishes for the tale in the translation by Richard F. Burton, 1885. Collinet (p. 280) mentions that a parody by the poet François Gacon was obscene.

[18] See Christiane Klapisch-Zuber, translated by Lydia G. Cochrane, *Women, Family and Ritual in Renaissance Italy*, Chicago: University of Chicago Press (1985), 229.

in print by other authors are often of the greatest importance: the Brothers Grimm in the nineteenth century, and before Perrault's time the Italians Giovanni Straparola and Giambattista Basile. Both compiled collections of stories, usually called novellas, taken from various sources. This was the genre founded by Boccaccio, whose style was followed closely by Straparola in the 1550s with his *Piacevoli notti* ('Entertaining Nights'). Basile's *Pentamerone* (1634–6), although the title recalls Boccaccio's, is further from him in its earthy, picturesque style. Both must have been sources for Perrault.[19]

To judge by an article about the *Contes* in the *Mercure galant* which almost certainly reflected Perrault's views,[20] he shared the stance on authorship commonly taken by students of folk-tale. The argument was that, although the authors of such works liked to be considered their inventors, it was really a matter of oral tradition: 'an infinite number of fathers and mothers, grandmothers, governesses and much-loved nannies, who for perhaps as long as a thousand years have contributed, each one improving on the one before, many entertaining circumstantial details which have been preserved, while anything ill-conceived has been forgotten'. As one in the long line of tellers, then, his aim would have been to 'improve on the one before', the versions he had heard or found in print, by adding details for entertainment and suppressing those deemed unsuitable or uninteresting. The process is perceptible in *Donkey-Skin*, where much if not all the humour comes from Perrault. The subject, however, must have been chosen in response to La Fontaine, who had written: 'If I were told of Donkey-Skin, | I'd listen with extreme delight.'[21] In Perrault's version, the tone and many of the incidents resemble those of *Three Silly Wishes* and are quite different from *Griselda*.

---

[19] This applies even though the language of the *Pentamerone* is a difficult Neapolitan dialect, which Perrault is unlikely to have read with any facility; it was not translated into French until after his death. He could have had the help of an intermediary.

[20] Collinet edition, p. 28. The argument was attributed to unspecified 'connoisseurs': very probably a disguise for Perrault, who was on good terms with the editor; the article would have been publicity for the *Contes*.

[21] 'Si Peau d'Ane m'était conté | J'y prendrais un plaisir extrême'; *Fables*, VIII. iv.

However, it shares some important elements with the earlier poem, since both have a Cinderella-like heroine who is found by a prince. Moreover, the last part of *Griselda* preserves the episode in Boccaccio's tale when it seems that the Prince might marry his daughter, only for him to reject the prospect at the last moment as 'a terrible fate'.

As La Fontaine implied, the Donkey-Skin story was a recognized part of contemporary folklore. The principal episodes—a widowed father who, failing to find another wife to match the first, announces that he wishes to marry his daughter; her flight, assisted by magic and in a degrading disguise; the meeting with a prince and the release from her lowly state through some magic token of love—are found in many traditional tales and written literature throughout the Middle Ages and the Renaissance. Perrault would have known the tale in outline, even if he had not heard it as a child. He might also have read the life of the Celtic St Dympna, who was martyred by her father for refusing his advances.[22] However, in contrast to *Griselda*, there is no religious dimension to his *Peau d'Âne*.

In the great repertoire of folk-tale known as Aarne-Thompson, now revised by Uther,[23] Donkey-Skin tales are given their own category, type 510B. Among the other versions listed are three from the important printed collections. Straparola, Basile, and the Brothers Grimm all have stories with a widowed king whose daughter flees from his approaches, and like Perrault's heroine performs domestic tasks for a prince, but the manner of their flight varies, as do the magical elements and the tasks they are set.[24] Straparola and Basile differ from Perrault in presenting their stories as historical anecdotes, despite the magic elements, which are a sign of folk-tale origin; in his treatment, as in the Grimms' version, it appears as legend. Perrault's humorous verse further distances his subject from reality. After the jokes about the donkey, it is that much harder to be seriously affected

[22] She figured in a well-known hagiographic work by the Portuguese writer Ribadaneira, *Flos sanctorum* ('The Flower of the Saints') often published in French translation during the seventeenth century. See Warner, *Beast to Blonde*, ch. 20.

[23] Antti Aarne, *The Types of the Folk Tale, A Classification and Bibliography*, revised and enlarged by Stith Thompson, 1961 (first edition 1928), but superseded since 2004 by Hans-Jörg Uther's further revision (see Select Bibliography).

[24] For further details see Appendix A, on *Donkey-Skin*.

by the heroine's plight, especially since her fairy godmother is shown to be a little inept in handling it. The character of her father is more mildly treated in Perrault than in Straparola, or in the legend of St Dympna, where both are out-and-out villains seeking murderous revenge on their daughters. In Perrault's time a king was semi-sacred, at any rate in public writings, and the father's lust is duly purified, in a scene worthy of the sentimental dénouements of eighteenth-century family dramas.

Despite all this, it remains striking that in *Donkey-Skin* the possibility of incest is treated openly, at least as far as adults are concerned. They will understand 'marriage' as a euphemism for sexual abuse, but for young children the implications remain hidden; small girls who announce, as commonly happens, that they will marry Daddy do not mean what adults mean. If the story is meant as a cautionary tale, like *Little Red Riding-Hood*, its openness has advantages. It becomes possible to include the opinions of minor characters who tell the heroine that she must resist her father's suggestion at all costs, a standard feature of the different versions. If you accept that girls should be warned against sexual abuse within the family, it is difficult to see how the warning can be given more explicitly without unacceptable detail. A related problem arises with a motif found in Perrault and the Grimms, but not the Italian collections: the three dresses and the animal's skin. These gifts demanded by the daughter have often been held to show that she is not wholeheartedly opposed to her father's approaches. To my mind, the argument is superficial. The gifts supply, first, the means to attract the suitor she wants when the time comes, and secondly, the ugly disguise which will deter any sexual approaches meanwhile.

## 3. The Tales in Prose

The term 'folk-tale' implies an adult audience; fairy-tale, a story for children. The distinction is familiar now, but in the past it scarcely existed. *Donkey-Skin* illustrates this. Many would be reluctant to give it to children nowadays, but from Perrault's Preface to the *Contes* it is evident that in the seventeenth century things were not the same;

women tell it to children as a matter of course, he remarks,[25] and his relative Mlle Lhéritier adds in her comments that she was delighted by it as a child. Basile in the 1630s put in his title that his stories are for children. The distinction between adult and children's literature was also blurred by La Fontaine, whose style brilliantly combines simplicity and sophistication; Perrault followed the same recipe in *Three Silly Wishes* and *Donkey-Skin*.

The prose tales, however, show a definite change. Most are clearly intended only for quite young children (though they are being read to by adults, no doubt), the exceptions being *Bluebeard* and *Ricky the Tuft*. In this respect they are distinct not only from the anonymous tales recounted from ancient times at gatherings of both adults and children in the unlit evenings or during communal work, but also from those by Perrault's contemporaries, Mme d'Aulnoy and others, who wrote 'contes merveilleux' (magic tales) for an adult readership. Perhaps the clearest example is *Little Red Riding-Hood*. Like another favourite of smaller children, *The Three Little Pigs*, it is halfway to being a game. It ends with the delicious mock-frightening ritualistic formulas, and (preferably) a hug from the storyteller at the words 'eat you with'. The manuscript copy spelt it out: 'You say these words loudly to frighten the child, as if the wolf were going to eat it.' The Moral, however, is separately addressed to grown-ups—a brief and witty equivalent of our Freudian interpretations.

Another feature distinguishing his tales from those published for adults at the same period is concision, notably exemplified in *Red Riding-Hood*. It is a basic virtue in tales for small children, and depends on simplicity, not easy to achieve. Much in the *Contes* that seems simple is from folk-tale, and is now considered typical of children's stories: the limited and conventional range of characters, kings and queens, princesses and princes, ogres and fairy godmothers, often morally unambiguous, completely good or completely bad.[26] They may be multiplied, but are never complicated: two hostile sisters, or

---

[25] 'The tale of Donkey-Skin is told to children, day in day out, by their governesses and grandmothers'; see below, p. 4.

[26] For a valuable discussion of this stylization and related topics, see Max Lüthi, *Once Upon a Time*, Bloomington: University of Indiana Press (1970), ch. 3.

brothers at the beginning of *Puss in Boots*, seven brothers including Hop. The same applies with repeated incidents: three wishes, three requests for dresses (though only two visits to the ball: many versions of *Cinderella* have three). The effect is to increase narrative tension. The technique is taken even further in *Bluebeard*, with the seemingly endless dialogue between the threatening villain, the victim, and her sister. This example also illustrates the formulaic moments of dialogue that are a feature of folk-tale and which Perrault seems carefully to have preserved. The directions from Red Riding-Hood's grandmother about opening the door are a particularly clear example, since they are in the language of the Middle Ages. They seem fixed and unalterable, but that is not always the case. At the end of *Red Riding-Hood* the dialogue with the wolf is found with many minor variations, and it is evident that narrators would have felt free to develop their own versions even of permanent elements in a tale.

However, Perrault chose at times to insert self-consciously literary elements in the *Contes*. He keeps the time-honoured opening, 'Il était une fois . . .' ('Once upon a time . . .'), but in the endings to two tales, *Hop o' my Thumb* and *Ricky the Tuft*, permits himself an authorial intervention, questioning whether what we have just heard is genuine. These passages look as if they were intended for more cultivated audiences than those who listened to grandmothers or village storytellers. For some critics, as with the knowing tone of some of the Morals, this sophistication spoils the naive charm of the stories—a fair comment on *Hop*, in my view, but not with *Ricky*, which throughout assumes in its hearers a high level of linguistic appreciation. More often, the passages which seem to be Perrault's own contributions are effective both for children and adults. He marks important moments in the action by tiny dramatic scenes: the wicked fairy's curse in *Sleeping Beauty*; the encounter on the path between wolf and grandchild; Bluebeard's tempting prohibition; and so on. Every tale contains significant and entertaining dialogue of this kind, and it is particularly noticeable in the tales in which speech itself is a vital part of the story, *Puss in Boots*, *The Fairies*, and *Ricky the Tuft*.

Among Perrault's greatest talents as a storyteller is his eye for memorable detail. Several of the most famous are in the titles, and it seems certain that he invented them: the red hood, the cat's boots, the glass slipper, the beard. Although there seem to be many, they are used sparingly. Only very occasionally does Perrault fall into a common fault in tales involving magic, which is to weaken its effect by overuse.[27] Probably the best examples are in the tale of tales, *Cinderella*, when in the transformation scene the godmother and Cinderella cooperate. It is a masterpiece of narrative partly because of the clever dialogue, which both moves the action forward and shows the little girl developing in maturity.[28] In addition, the objects that the two discuss have great symbolic value: the magical transformation of humble or unpleasant domestic things into the glamorous trappings of court life foretells the change from persecuted child to attractive young woman.

In this case, the magic objects can be interpreted without reference to sexual symbolism, but more often the opposite is true. Many if not all the vivid details I have mentioned, and the scenes in which they occur, are usually explicated with reference to sexuality. Thus the old woman's spindle on which Sleeping Beauty pricks her finger is not only a picturesque item in the narrative but a sexual symbol, its swelling shape suggesting a woman rather than a girl. More obscurely, although from Perrault himself onwards commentators have been virtually unanimous on the point, Red Riding-Hood's encounter with the wolf symbolizes the sexual act, the colour of the hood implying from the outset that she is, at least potentially, a sexual being.

Caution is required in symbolic analysis; it is not enough, as is sometimes assumed, to equate symbol to reality in a one-to-one relationship and leave it at that. Things are usually more complicated. Bluebeard's beard is a masculine symbol, yes, as Donkey-Skin's ring is a female one; but whereas in her story a sexual implication can

---

[27] Two possible counter-examples: in *Sleeping Beauty* there is no real need for the dwarf with seven-league boots and the fairy's flying chariot; nor for the apparition of the cooks from underground in *Ricky the Tuft*. This resembles the dance interludes common in theatrical entertainments in Perrault's time, but contributes little to the story apart from recalling the underground kingdom of the goblins, the origin of Ricky no doubt being the figure of the Goblin King (see Collinet's edition, p. 290).

[28] As she does throughout the tale: in the scene with her sisters after she returns from the ball she has already become aware of her own privileged position.

clearly be seen when she hides her ring in the cake intended for the Prince,[29] it is not at all clear why the beard is blue, and commentators have offered many explanations. Later in the tale, the symbolism becomes even more enigmatic. Even in *Donkey-Skin*, there are problems with the somewhat comic animal ('the beast so pure | That what he dropped was not manure . . .') and its skin; the association of excrement with wealth is common in folklore, and a donkey often symbolizes crude male desire, but it would probably be wrong to look for any exact meaning here: the associations are effective while remaining vague. However, it does seem that the killing of the donkey corresponds to the destruction of the threat from Donkey-Skin's father.

As with Freudian theories in general, there is commonly some reluctance to accept that stories which seem innocent and charming, like children, contain a substratum of meaning which is neither. Many parents are like Sleeping Beauty's father, who seemingly wants to preserve her from sexuality. However, whether or not Freudian analysis is correct in affirming that children are already sexual beings, there is no doubt that, however charming, they are destined to become so. Virtually all the symbolism in Perrault's tales points to the conclusion that one of the underlying subjects is this great transition in human development. Another is the more general process of growth away from dependence on parents.

This is the basis for an interpretation of fairy-tale which has had very wide influence, that of Bruno Bettelheim in his *The Uses of Enchantment*.[30] Fairy-tale in general, he argues, is concerned not simply with growing up, but with the manifold anxieties, often deeply felt and disturbing, to which children are subject as their development continues. The function of the stories is to provide imaginative reassurance that the process will not result in disaster but end 'happily ever after'. Thus fairy-tale should evoke fears, but also show how

---

[29] Though even here there is sufficient reason in the narrative for her to hide it; the sexual innuendo is additional, not essential.

[30] Subtitled *The Meaning and Importance of Fairy Tales*, New York: Knopf (1976); see for example p. 5. Devotees of Perrault have to allow for a degree of prejudice against him in what Bettelheim says.

they may be surmounted. There are reservations to be made about Bettelheim's work, especially over the detail of his commentaries on individual tales, but his theory in outline convincingly explains both why the content of so many of them is unpleasant, and why they have an important role to play in ensuring children's psychological health. Few adults would deny, even if they do not remember it in themselves, that children suffer what seem unwarranted and exaggerated anxieties, about both their present circumstances and the future, or that they are often in open or concealed conflict with parents and siblings, while remaining deeply attached to them. Fairy-tales, which children know to be unreal, permit them vicariously to confront fears and indulge feelings they recognize as bad but cannot avoid: fears of rejection by parents, for instance, in *Hop o' my Thumb*, or hostility to parent and sister in *Cinderella*. The freedom to feel with Hop or Cinderella is the greater because their circumstances are amplified by fantasy: the ordinary resentments of childhood, if realistically reproduced, would not offer the same emotional depth as the extreme situations of fairy-tale. Bettelheim stresses the greater imaginative force and value of seemingly unrealistic fairy-tales as compared with rational discourse or the dull realism of much fiction for children.

At the same time, the stories make positive suggestions about resolving anxieties and conflicts. A bad mother-figure, in the shape of Cinderella's stepmother, is superseded by a good one when her godmother appears, leaving the child free to believe that, somehow, the mother it is cross with and by whom it is persecuted will disappear and be replaced by a kinder one. In *Hop o' my Thumb* the progression is different. The parent-figures in the second part are even more threatening than the 'real' parents of the first part (though in relation to each other they are the same: the mother less cruel than the father), but Hop's cleverness gets him and his brothers out of their predicament, and, very quickly, brings success in the wider world. The obvious message, put openly in the Morals, is that attractiveness and kindness for girls, and intelligence and bravery for boys, are valuable qualities. Since we like to believe that we possess them, the message is likely to prove acceptable.

A specific problem in interpreting *Cinderella* is raised by its association with *Donkey-Skin* in folklore studies.[31] Comparing the two shows at once that the outline of *Cinderella* is to be found in the later parts of *Donkey-Skin*. The main difference, of course, lies in the family relationships: the father is largely or completely excluded from Cinderella stories. He is either dead or powerless against the second wife, and the persecution of the heroine is due not to him, but the other females in the family. This suggests that, in the history of the tale (at least as regards Perrault's version) the original plotline was that of *Donkey-Skin*, and that at some point the outline story of *Cinderella* became separated from the incidents that precede it in *Donkey-Skin*. The result is that Perrault's *Cinderella* does not contain any reference to incestuous child-abuse. For Perrault, then, as for Basile before him, the two tales are distinct. If the prose *Cinderella* is a romanticized fantasy for children about growing up, the verse *Donkey-Skin*, with its franker treatment of the sexual side, is a straightforward cautionary tale, the fairy openly describing the father's desires as wrong.

*Sleeping Beauty*, *The Fairies*, and *Ricky*, together with the more difficult *Red Riding-Hood* and *Bluebeard*, are other tales manifestly directed towards girl children which concern the normal processes of maturation. The symbolism in *Sleeping Beauty*, as I have mentioned, transforms the onset of puberty into the famous spinning-wheel incident. The later piece of magic, the barrier of trees that is effective against all except her future husband, implies a long period of chastity before the first sexual experience, which in Perrault, unlike his best-known predecessors, is equated with marriage. In later versions this is where the tale concludes, making it an ideal allegory of bourgeois mating rituals: children protected, sexuality reluctantly conceded, but hidden, then a refusal to allow anyone except one worthy suitor to approach. The Grimms' version adds some rivals to point the lesson, but ends with marriage.

In the later part of Perrault's version, Beauty's role becomes that of the wife in a clandestine marriage, a not uncommon event in France

---

[31] Both are type 510 in Aarne-Thompson-Uther (following Marian Roalfe Cox's work of 1893). ATU simply calls type 510A Cinderella and type 510B by Perrault's title Peau d'Âne.

at the time. It becomes necessary to hide the offspring from the mother-in-law, who behaves (leaving her ogreish propensities aside) like any other mother who suspects that her son is having an illicit affair. The story's subject, then, has changed, and now concerns the notoriously difficult relationship between a man's wife and his mother—perhaps not a topic that might be expected in a fairy-tale. We can reconstruct the reasons for it by comparing Perrault's tale with Basile's earlier version. Here, the Prince who finds the sleeping Talia is already married, and takes advantage of her unconscious state to father twins on her; in due course, the jealous wife finds out, and seeks a dreadful revenge, exactly like Beauty's mother-in-law. But when Perrault was writing, propriety forbade that a princess should suffer virtual rape. Perrault makes the Prince behave honourably—though the marriage takes place with suspicious haste—but then has to face the problem that there is no convenient jealous wife to act as villain. The traditionally troublesome figure of the mother-in-law comes to the rescue, though at some cost to narrative plausibility.[32]

*Little Red Riding-Hood*, *The Fairies*, and *Ricky the Tuft* treat the subject of growing up with a greater or lesser degree of magic symbolism. The warnings, reassurance, or advice they contain seem to be intended for different age-groups. Only in the first, for the youngest, does the symbolism present serious problems. In each, the advice seems obvious (though not quite what the Morals say): do not talk to strange men; be nice to your elders, even if they are poor; and remember that looks are not everything, intelligent conversation counts as well. *Ricky*, the longest, needs its length in order to give examples of what is meant; it is designed for young women of the later seventeenth century in France, with its *précieux* traditions of elegant talk, often flirtatious, in the salons where articulate women dominated. It is also, no doubt, a weaker, polite version of tales of the 'Frog Prince' type, in which the future husband appears first as repugnant, the animal suitors symbolically representing fears about the physical side

[32] It is interesting that in a much older version, the Ninth Captain's Tale in *The 1001 Nights*, things are more relaxed: the affair between prince and beautiful girl is only slightly worrying for his mother, who collaborates with her to make the union permanent. See Appendix A.

of sex.[33] *The Fairies*, by contrast, must be for a young audience, old enough to appreciate that the unkind sister is 'rude', as children say, but not enough to object to the scarcely disguised nannyish advice.

*Little Red Riding-Hood* is difficult not only because it has been made so by commentators, who often speculate about the complicity of the little girl in her seduction, if seduction it is, but also because there are widely differing versions, of which that by the Brothers Grimm, in which the wolf is killed, has tended to supersede Perrault's.[34] Killing the wolf seems appropriate for a cautionary tale, seriously warning about real wolves in the countryside, but Perrault's Moral, making the wolf symbolic, suggests that in Paris the threat of actually being eaten was no longer felt to be serious. Indeed, it is hard to understand why the bed scene would have been devised if the 'wolf' was only wanting food. If the intention was to tell the story to small girls, then a simple explanation seems to be best: a warning that males—whatever else he is, the wolf is male—may do awful things to girl children. That sexual danger is meant will be apparent to adults, as with the marriage in *Donkey-Skin*, but for the limited understanding of the child it is transformed into another dreadful fate. The enjoyable series of questions and answers at the end, nonetheless, seems to me ambiguous, more subtly so than is sometimes assumed: it shows the danger but, by turning the dialogue into a kind of game, suggests that it is not entirely real, leaving the way open for the child to develop her own understanding of what is involved.

Those who know other versions of *Red Riding-Hood* may find this too simple. Many versions collected from rural France in the nineteenth century and later contain puzzling and gruesome elements which had been lost to sight to polite society. Among them are the two routes that the girl can take, the 'path of pins' and the 'path of needles'; explicated in terms of the rural culture of the time, they

---

[33] Aarne-Thompson Type 440, the animal bridegroom. In this, Perrault's version is distinct from the two contemporary literary tales to which it must be related, by Mlle Lhéritier and Mlle Bernard (see Appendix A), since in them the idea that the woman is reconciled to the man's ugliness is not found.

[34] A further example of the tendency to eliminate the 'nastiness' of fairy-tale is to be found in a recent version of *Red Riding-Hood* published in the Ladybird series: the wolf survives to become vegetarian.

symbolize successive stages in her life, first when she can have suitors, and then the stage of sexual activity.[35] As for the wolf, sometimes called a werewolf, he consumes the grandmother but keeps back some flesh and blood which he tells the girl to cook and eat, which she does (sometimes being warned what she is doing; sometimes reluctantly). Incongruously, when in bed, she escapes by saying that she must go outside to relieve herself. The wolf tells her to 'do it in the bed', but she insists. It is entirely probable that, despite the lapse of two hundred years, versions with such motifs come virtually unaltered from Perrault's time, or well before, and that in *Le Petit Chaperon rouge* we have a story which has been cleaned up, either by Perrault himself or some previous teller.

Despite this, *Red Riding-Hood* is easy enough to comprehend on the surface at least, both for child and adult. *Bluebeard*, by contrast, has always seemed both terrifying and mysterious. Although his wife is rescued, the tension generated by the wait for her brothers leaves behind it the sense that the dangers cannot be simply forgotten. But what is her sin, exactly? The literalist view—that it is mere inquisitiveness—cannot be taken seriously, despite Perrault's first Moral (itself tongue-in-cheek); the punishment is too severe. Marina Warner, however, has a wealth of material to show that in Victorian times the tale was taken to warn, with enthusiasm, of the dangers of curiosity,[36] as if the commentators were on Bluebeard's side. This tendency was foreshadowed in a Christianized variant recorded by the Grimms, *Our Lady's Child*, which keeps the heroine's curiosity but removes the context of marriage; a girl adopted by the Virgin is cruelly punished for a sin analogous to that of Bluebeard's wife. She admits her sin at the last moment, which saves her from being burnt alive.

Disregarding this, what Bluebeard forbids his wife must be some kind of sexual knowledge or act, shown symbolically; what it is has

---

[35] See an article by Yvonne Verdier, often reproduced or summarized: 'Grands-mères, si vous saviez: *Le Petit Chaperon rouge* dans la tradition orale', *Cahiers de la littérature orale*, 4 (1978); and Appendix A on *Red Riding-Hood* below.

[36] *Beast to Blonde*, 244–6. Some of the comments she records make a connection with the sin of Eve, desire for sexual knowledge; but Eve was a virgin, unlike—presumably—Bluebeard's wife.

been interpreted in various ways, all open to serious objections. Perhaps the commonest view follows Freud: the key and the lock symbolize the sexual act. Hence the dead wives show what will happen to the new wife if she is unfaithful, and the ineradicable blood shows that infidelity cannot be concealed. In favour of this view is the likelihood that a wife would be warned against it, that Bluebeard's departure provides an obvious opportunity, and that jealous husbands were frequently violent if adultery was proved; against it, that the wife is not actually unfaithful—unless the key and lock are taken to represent it; but then, there is no lover. Nonetheless, Bluebeard behaves as if she had been unfaithful, like, presumably, all the other wives. In the terms of the story, what she has done is to yield to the temptation he deliberately places before her; it must therefore be meant as a test.

The other problem is that, if the wife has been guilty, she gets away with it. Among the many other versions of the tale, some stress the monstrosity or devilishness of the husband, thus justifying the wife's escape. Other, less closely related versions, say that Bluebeard kills his wives if they become pregnant. This is the tradition preserved in a saint's life from Brittany, a region long connected with Bluebeard. The saint's life might not be especially relevant except that medieval frescoes illustrating it correspond exactly to scenes in Perrault's tale: the marriage, the handing over of a key, a room in which seven dead wives are hanging, and Bluebeard's attempt to murder his wife.[37]

The efforts that have been made to unravel the obscure but powerful symbolism tend to preserve the assumption that Bluebeard's wife is at fault, but it is of course he who is the villain, and several times over, so it seems: a serial killer. The lesson to draw, then, might be very simple, that girls should avoid marrying sinister men, even if, or perhaps especially if, they possess great wealth. Mothers too should find a lesson here, the girl's mother having taken no notice of the warning signs. *Bluebeard* is not quite an anti-*Cinderella* in the sense that it warns against marriage in general—the wife remarries

---

[37] Warner, *Beast to Blonde*, 261. She comments that the pictures 'anticipate very satisfyingly the fairytale ogre, as chronicled by Perrault'.

happily—but it certainly makes clear that there may be dangers involved.

The two tales for boys, *Hop o' my Thumb* and *Puss in Boots*, are distinct in that the symbolism usually does not concern sex, while the message conveyed by the success of the heroes is naturally about the worldly qualities considered valuable for men, courage and ingenuity rather than beauty and charm (though Perrault in one of the Morals is not above pointing out that masculine attractiveness may also be useful). *Hop o' my Thumb*, though less skilful as narration than *Puss*, is the more disturbing, in that it openly deals with a terrible idea, the possibility of being eaten. Do we therefore interpret the tale (and its more successful version from the Brothers Grimm, *Hansel and Gretel*) as being basically a resolution of such anxiety? To do so involves believing that children do in fact suffer from this fear, and that the story does not only magnify the fear of rejection.[38] The threat of being eaten is of course a common theme both in folk-tale generally and in stories for children; the Grimms' *The Juniper Tree* is another well-known example. Often the threat comes from an ogre, defined by Perrault as 'a savage man who ate small children',[39] but more usually thought of as a giant, as in the English tale of Jack the Giant-Killer.

If children are indeed afraid of being eaten, if only in nightmares, the person they fear must be an adult, who is in the same relation of size to a child as a giant is to men. Bettelheim records the response of a 5-year-old boy to his mother after she had told him the tale of Jack the Giant-Killer: 'There aren't such things as giants, are there? . . . But there are such things as grownups, and they're like giants.'[40] In Perrault, the terrifying idea is somewhat mitigated by the division of the story into two parts (rather like the division in *Sleeping Beauty*,

[38] This is Bettelheim's view (*The Uses of Enchantment*), it seems; curiously, he says very little about the fear of cannibalism. See his discussion of *Hansel and Gretel*, especially p. 166 on the witch being a 'fantastically exaggerated' personification of the child's 'immature dread'.

[39] Note to the dedicatory lines in *Donkey-Skin*; below, p. 52. The reason for the past tense 'ate' is probably that ogres are supposed to belong to times past.

[40] Bettelheim, *Uses of Enchantment*, 27. He mentions that the mother knew that her son had fantasies about cannibalism, and like many parents was doubtful of the wisdom of telling her child a tale containing horrific elements.

where an equally horrifying episode is kept until the second part). In the first, the parents, faced with starvation, prefer to abandon the children in the forest rather than to watch them die; it is in the second and more fantastic section that the fear of being eaten is made explicit, and the danger does not come from a parent, but from a monstrous stranger. Assuming that Perrault's source was a tale of the 'Mother Killed Me, Father Ate Me' type, he converted what must be the most terrible fear of all into something marginally less so (as did the Grimms with the witch): the threat comes from a being who can, as it were, safely be defeated because he is a monster, and the child can identify comfortingly with the dauntless hero. When Perrault published the *Contes*, the possibility of being eaten was not pure fantasy, since widespread and serious famine had recently occurred, which must have made the implications in *Hop o' my Thumb* worse than they probably appear now.

*Puss in Boots* is the boy's counterpart of a Cinderella story—the hero-victim suffers less from his family, but is in sad straits nonetheless when a magic helper appears and brings about, in stages, a transformation analogous to that in *Cinderella*; poor orphan boy marries princess and becomes rich. However, there is virtually no sexual symbolism; the young man's concealment naked in the river before meeting the Princess is suggestive enough in itself.[41] Most of the symbolism in the tale conceals the same terrors as in *Hop o' my Thumb*, but again in mitigated form: the being who may be eaten is not the boy, but Puss, momentarily endangered at the beginning. When the same danger arises in the Ogre's castle, Puss has already proved so resourceful that it seems to be just another problem to be ingeniously overcome.

Puss's stratagems are often criticized for being merely deceitful, and the tale as a whole is clearly not edifying. It belongs more to the picaresque tradition in literature, stories of the enterprising rascal whose tricks are endearing rather than regrettable. There are also echoes of another ancient tradition, this time aristocratic, that of the

---

[41] Although we are told by Freudian analysis that water is one of the commonest symbols of sexual activity.

clever valet whose ruses assist a noble master, the master himself necessarily being honourable; he can benefit from the servant's lack of
scruple but not instigate it.[42] Puss's lies, as Louis Marin showed in his
analysis of the tale,[43] are of a remarkable kind: they become true
largely because telling them helps to make them true. Puss's announce-
ments about the Marquis of Carabas—with some contributions of his
own—convince everyone that the young man is indeed a nobleman.
Only then does he progressively acquire the necessary perquisites, a
princess, an estate, and a castle. However, they are acquired in the
wrong order, so to speak. In reality, a young man of merit rising
through society would have made his fortune first, then bought
estates, then married; only at a late stage would he be ennobled and
given a title. But Puss's plan assumes that if the title is given—by
him—all the rest will follow, and to our delight it does.

In other words the attraction of the story is that it is almost pure
entertainment: the lightest of the *Contes*, and one of the most skilful.
What then of Perrault's claim, in the Preface, that in all the tales the
primary purpose was didactic? The narrative, he said, was simply an
envelope for 'une morale utile', a useful moral lesson. This was conventional. The function of literature was invariably defined, in French
theoretical writing, as a combination of the 'useful' and the 'pleasant',
a formula that went back to Horace; few were those who even suggested that their main purpose was simply to entertain. In Perrault's
case, however, the argument that the tales are morally instructive is
undermined by the Morals themselves, which are more often than not
unserious. To critics they have often seemed frivolous or cynical.
Certainly they contain a good deal of irony, which often goes unap-
preciated by the more solemn commentators. The conclusion of
*Bluebeard*, for instance, is the remark that the modern husband is
not a tyrant, but 'quiet as a mouse', which (in view of some other

[42] Perhaps the most familiar, though very late, example is Figaro in his first incar-
nation, in Beaumarchais's *Barber of Seville*.

[43] The chapter 'A la Conquête du pouvoir' in *Le Récit est un piège*, Paris: Les
Éditions de Minuit (1978), included as 'Recipes for Power' in *Food for Thought*, trans-
lation by Mette Hjort of his *La Parole mangée*, Baltimore: Johns Hopkins University
Press (1997).

anti-feminist passages) is likely to be read as a masculine jibe at the modern wife rather than a comment on the story. *Donkey-Skin* ends with several 'moral' observations, some resembling the *Bluebeard* Moral, some so trite as to be meaningless ('whatever trials life may send | Virtue will triumph in the end'). When the comments seem to be meant seriously, as with *Cinderella*, *The Fairy*, and *Puss in Boots*, they are prudential, that is, they concern the qualities that are needed to avoid risks and get on in the world, justifying self-interest rather than altruism. This is another way in which Perrault resembles La Fontaine, and like him he may use the Moral to make remarks which are not merely repetitions of what has just been expressed in the story. The second Moral to *Ricky*, for example, makes a common but worthwhile point about the nature of love.

The general impression given by the Morals, however, is that Perrault was seeking to distance himself and his adult readers from the more uncomfortable aspects of the stories. No Moral deals directly with the brutality which confronts the characters, whether from ogres, parents, or husbands. It is as if adults, rather than children, need to be protected from the ugly side of life. The same impression comes from considering the function of the symbolism. When the basic subject is cannibalism, or the risk of being eaten, the idea is disguised; the potential victim becomes an animal (Puss), or the aggressor a non-human being, an ogre or ogress. When sex is the subject, it is concealed by symbolic objects. Even where it is difficult to say what the symbols mean specifically, as in *Bluebeard*, there can be little doubt about the general implication. Again, in considering the probable revisions made by Perrault, it looks as though the purpose was to exclude or alter the more unpleasant episodes. The clearest cases are *Sleeping Beauty* and *Red Riding-Hood*, from which episodes known in other versions, such as the Prince's violation of the unconscious girl and the wolf's treatment of the grandmother's corpse, are absent; if Perrault knew them, as seems probable, he must have decided against them on the grounds that they would be found offensive, and made the necessary alterations.

The result of all this is that the tales in prose, at least—the position is different with those in verse—became suited to the middle-class sensibilities of his time. These, so it would appear, did not alter fundamentally for centuries, despite some changes in Victorian times, when the classic fairy-tale text became the Grimms' collection. As regards morality, in the widest sense of the word, Perrault's stories seem to have been considered still relevant. Nor would their rural setting have seemed unfamiliar, when even town dwellers were still accustomed to the traditions of an agricultural society. Late in the nineteenth century came more significant changes. This is the time when Thomas Hardy's novels were recording a world in which folktale would still have been a normal part of life, but which was not to last much longer. Perrault himself had made out, although the decor of the tales was that of his own time, that they came from a vaguely medieval past. By the middle of the twentieth century, his pretence of antiquity had become a reality. Even the medium of print was being superseded by electronic communications, just as print had superseded oral tradition.

It is common to lament the passing of fairy-tale as a consequence of these changes. In 1946 Stith Thompson said that 'folktale has gone the way of the bow and arrow'.[44] However, it may be too early to pronounce it dead. Writers of books and makers of films go on using characters and plots from Perrault's tales and others. We should perhaps accept that fairy-tales from the past have to be put into modern forms in order to be appreciated; that is preferable to oblivion. Perrault himself claimed to be doing no more, and no less, than countless other narrators who took stories they knew and presented them afresh. La Fontaine wrote, in the dedication to his second collection of fables, that a story 'truly casts a spell', because it 'makes a captive of the soul'. Who would disagree? Those by Perrault have held a good few people spellbound over the centuries and we may reasonably suppose that they will go on doing so. For the majority among us, readers and listeners who lack the creative gift, it is to be hoped that they will also inspire others to follow his example.

[44] *The Folktale*, New York: Dryden (1946) (quoted from the 1977 edition (Berkeley and Los Angeles: University of California Press), 461).

# NOTE ON THE TEXT
# AND TRANSLATION

AN asterisk in the text signifies a note at the back of the book.

There is no question about the choice of text to follow: the only full text is that of the 1697 edition of the *Histoires ou Contes*, left unrevised by Perrault. As regards variants, there are significant differences only for *Sleeping Beauty* and *The Fairies*, on which see Appendix B, although the 1695 manuscript contains numerous variant readings of minor importance. I have mainly used the edition by Collinet, but have frequently consulted also those by Rouger and Soriano (the latter being the only one to give all the variant readings). All provide much assistance with seventeenth-century meanings and the biographical, historical, and literary background.

I have usually left the traditional titles untouched, except for *Ricky the Tuft*, which is better than the unidiomatic *Ricky with the Tuft*. For *Le Petit Poucet* I have preferred *Hop o' my Thumb* to *Little Thumbling*, the common alternative. (Tom Thumb is a different character.) The only verse tale title calling for comment is *Three Silly Wishes*, the standard alternative *The Foolish Wishes* having, I think, too much alliteration. Children's editions of the tales are often given the general title 'Tales of Mother Goose' or similar; *Contes de ma mère l'oie* was not used by Perrault himself except in the 1695 manuscript of the first five tales, although the words are to be seen in the frontispiece of the 1697 *Contes*, and has been so often used for other collections that a less quaint title seemed preferable.

I believe this to be the first complete English translation in which verse is rendered in verse. The full *Griselidis* has never been translated, as far as I know. Usually all or some of the verse tales, when they are included, are put into prose. The Morals which Perrault added to the prose tales are sometimes translated into verse, sometimes into prose. Of the prose tales, the first English translation is now generally attributed, following the Opies (*The Classic Fairy Tales*,

24 n. 1), to Robert Samber, in 1729: *Histories, or Tales of Past Times. By M. Perrault.* However, the old attribution to Guy Miège is still common in library catalogues. Samber's translation is probably the most commonly reprinted, under varying titles. It is lively and picturesque, but none too reliable as regards meaning, and was accurately revised by J. E. Mansion in *The Fairy Tales of Charles Perrault* (London: Harrap, 1922; reprinted as *Charles Perrault's Classic Fairy Tales*, London: Chancellor, 1986); here *Three Wishes* and *Donkey-Skin* are adapted for prose. There have been many other translations and innumerable adaptations, among which I have benefited from the translations or adaptations by Geoffrey Brereton (Harmondsworth: Penguin Books, 1957) and Neil Philip and Nicolette Simborowski (under the title *Little Red Riding Hood*, but including all the tales; London: Pavilion, s.d.). Angela Carter, *The Fairy Tales of Charles Perrault* (London: Gollancz, 1977), includes *Three Wishes* and *Donkey-Skin* in prose; the translation is loose, but moves well. I have as far as possible avoided consulting other translations, and may well have missed some that should be mentioned; many appear among the countless editions of single tales or selections.

My primary concern has been fidelity to the original meaning, but without sacrificing readability, bearing in mind that Perrault must originally have intended his stories to be read to children. In the prose tales, the language is usually simple, no doubt for the sake of effective narration, but is not without subtleties, and has greater variation in register than is sometimes supposed. Sometimes the simplicity of the vocabulary can be misleading. Often the meanings of words have changed, to a greater or lesser degree, and it is all too easy to assume that one understands a word without realizing what has changed. The verb *penser*, now 'to think', was often used to mean 'almost to do something': Bluebeard's wife did not really 'think that' she was breaking her neck as she ran downstairs, or (a moment or two later) that she was dying of fright: in English she 'nearly' did so. Again, the nasty sister in *The Fairies* is said to be 'brutale' at one point, meaning not that she was brutal, or even rough, but merely impolite and inconsiderate. On this matter I owe a debt of gratitude to French editors, who have done all the hard work of checking in seventeenth-century dictionaries.

Like his immediate predecessors Molière and La Fontaine, Perrault had an ear for colloquial speech, including that of children, and seems to have enjoyed reproducing it when opportunities arose, as with Red Riding-Hood's exchanges with the wolf or Cinderella's with her sisters. Here the translator should employ a different register from that required in *Ricky the Tuft*, where the conversation (apart from when the Princess is still stupid) is in courtly or salon mode, the measured elegance of Mme de Lafayette's characters in *La Princesse de Clèves*, which Perrault was probably imitating. In *The Fairies* it is of course essential to try to reproduce the politeness of the kind sister and the coarseness of the unkind one; if I have overdone it, I plead good intentions.

In the narrative sections Perrault quite often employs colloquial turns of phrase, as in the opening of *Sleeping Beauty*. However, the problem I have found in his narrative prose is not to do with register, but syntax. It seems likely that children at the end of the seventeenth century were expected to cope with more complex sentences than are usual today. His syntax is difficult by modern standards, and I have frequently felt the need to simplify it. Like most writers of his time, he arranges his sentences hierarchically: there is one main verb, the clause in which it appears being preceded and followed by rank upon rank, or so it sometimes seems, of subordinate clauses, introduced by whos and althoughs and so on. English often prefers to join clauses in the same sentence with conjunctions, and, but: 'and he' not 'who', 'but' not 'although', or else will split what might become a lengthy sentence into two or more. It is remarkable that even when he is using complicated constructions Perrault's narrative moves rapidly and smoothly; I have tried to keep its virtues, but am all too aware that I have often stumbled after him.

Generally, my views on translating from French have been much influenced by Jean-Paul Vinay and Jean Darbelnet's *Stylistique comparée du français et de l'anglais* (1958; available in English since 1995), an invaluable survey of the many diverse ways in which the two languages differ in idiom, not only as regards single words or phrases, but also at the level of clauses or even whole sentences. (My remarks just now about French and English sentences derive from this book.)

It is an essential corrective to the naive view that each word in French corresponds exactly, or even approximately, to a word in English—I have already given an example of this: the un-English title *Ricky with the Tuft* for *Riquet à la houppe*—and tends to argue that translation is more a matter of adapting content written in one language to the repertoire that the other language provides. This used to be taken for granted when ancient Latin or Greek had to be put into modern English, or vice versa for some persecuted students, but now it is a lesson that has to be learned afresh.

When the original is in verse, problems and priorities are rather different. Fidelity to the sense remains important, but poetry is not written mainly to convey an exact sense. The sound of words is also important, especially, of course, in rhyming poetry, and relates the words to each other in a manner independent of sense. Moreover the rhythm of verse ensures heavier emphasis on some syllables than on others, giving them greater significance. It is therefore a misapprehension to suppose that a prose translation will be the most faithful. To neglect the aesthetic appeal of metre and rhyme is at least as much of a betrayal as, with prose, it would be to rewrite rather than to translate. Besides that, in verse originals the style differs from that habitual in prose; even when the author avoids poetic diction the language of verse is usually more concentrated, which is why prose translations of verse are almost inevitably strained and unnatural. Even poorly turned verse is, I hope, better than the unreadability that easily results when a 'literal' prose translation is made. Conversely, the lift that rhyme and metre can give even to quite dull meanings justifies almost any attempt—and there have been some pretty bad ones—to keep the attractions of verse.

French is more generous with its rhymes than English, partly because its words are invariably stressed (though more lightly than in English) on the last syllable, and partly because it has a multitude of words ending in homophonous suffixes such as -age, -eur, -ant (or -ent), -elle, and many others. This is particularly true of the rather abstract language of the seventeenth century. It is some compensation that modern English has a wider vocabulary, rich in what are called concrete words. The result is often that the English sentence gives a

more abrupt and down-to-earth impression than its more lucid and
elegant French counterpart. This is not necessarily a disadvantage
when the verse is humorous, but when it is measured and stately, as in
many passages of *Griselidis*, the English version can all too easily turn
awkward and high-flown; I have done what I can to avoid it. French
is also quite at ease with the rhetorical style, often cultivated deliberately, which English is not, preferring the rhythms of the common
language. Perrault offers his own example in the early passage in
*Griselidis* when the orator exhorts the Prince to take a wife and the
Prince responds more naturally. Even so, in much that relates to the
Prince the style—of a type cultivated assiduously by Perrault and
many others in an epoch obsessed with grandeur—may well seem
pompous rather than eloquent. When the tone is less elevated, as in
the other two verse tales and the Morals, it is correspondingly easier
to convey the ironic or simply comic effects that he aims at.

Perrault was not a great poet, but he was a very good one. He
wrote easily in verse—he said that from his schooldays he preferred
it to writing prose—and could produce almost any style, precious,
lyrical, reflective, grandiloquent, or humorous, as required. The kind
which seems to have come most naturally to him was light and mildly
satirical, often making fun of his subjects but without malice, as in
*Three Wishes*. In the verse tales he follows La Fontaine's Fables in
using what passed for free verse at the time, that is, obeying the
numerous strict rules on rhyme which seventeenth-century conven-
tion imposed on poets, but mixing lines of varying lengths, twelve,
ten, or eight syllables, and occasionally indulging in a triple rhyme
rather than the pairs (in different combinations, aabb, abab, abba,
varied at will) which were normal. The English line of verse is normally measured by 'feet', iambic or dactylic (combining one stressed
and one unstressed, or one stressed and two unstressed—to put it
unprofessionally), usually in fives for a more serious tone, the famous
iambic pentameter, or in fours for lighter effects—though Andrew
Marvell used the tetrameter for both. I have mixed these two lengths
of line, as Perrault does, and varied the rhyme-scheme as he does, but
without trying to reproduce the patterns of his verse except occasionally. Nor have I observed anything like the invariable French rule of

alternating pairs of feminine rhymes (those ending in -e, now unsounded) with masculine (those ending otherwise). The only possible English counterpart for the feminine rhyme is the two-syllable rhyme, such as relation/situation; it almost always sounds overdone, although it can be excellent when humour is called for.

The verse Morals to the tales in prose call for separate consideration. They are mostly short, usually only a few lines, which increases the difficulty for the translator. Nor do I think it is unfair to Perrault to say that they are not among his own highest achievements; the best writing is also easier to translate. (It was only after I had decided that they could be rendered more or less satisfactorily into English that I felt justified in trying the longer poems.) With the Morals, the translator's ambition must be limited to giving an adequate rather than a good rendering. It was useful to be able to resort to the dactylic rhythm at times: it gives a few more syllables to play with. Although I hope not to have altered the sense in any significant respect, I should say, seeing that the Morals are so often the object of criticism, that only the French originals ought to be taken as the basis for comment on what Perrault might have intended.

There are a few important passages in which Perrault wrote what might be called, anachronistically, prose poetry. The main examples are the almost ritual formulas, printed in italics in the French editions, when Bluebeard's wife is calling to her sister and Puss addresses the country labourers. From the evidence of similar passages in other folk-tales, these appear to be traditional elements in the stories, religiously preserved by tellers (like the Old French employed by the grandmother in *Little Red Riding-Hood*), but there is no means of knowing. Wherever they came from, the language is poetic rather than prosaic, even if Puss's orders are rather fierce, and it seemed right to look for rhythmic and alliterative effects in English. Here, I fear, the wish may have to make do for the deed; it proved extremely hard to find anything that matched the flow of the words in French. Fortunately the other ritual formulas, the traditional opening 'Il était une fois' and others such as 'je vous donne pour don' ('I give you as gift'; copied from Samber), or Red Riding-Hood's exclamations in bed, are not as difficult because the English equivalents have been settled long ago and it is simply a matter of occasional fine tuning.

Briefly on the illustrations: the tales have been illustrated many times, but never more sympathetically or spectacularly than by Gustave Doré (1832–83), who illustrated many literary texts including Dante's *Inferno*, in 1861. He produced forty-one engravings for Hetzel's edition, *Les Contes de Perrault* (1867), from which the selection in this edition is taken. The Opies (*The Classic Fairy Tales*, 134) note that the 'masterly but horrific' plate of the Ogre in *Hop o' my Thumb*, when about to cut his daughters' throats, was omitted from the English edition.

There remains the pleasant duty of acknowledging the personal help I have had. My editor Judith Luna has been extraordinarily attentive to a whole series of matters (including the illustrations) which together add up to a very large contribution indeed. There have been times when I have wondered if it would have been better if she had undertaken the translation. She has made the volume as a whole better than it would otherwise have been, and has saved me from many slips and blunders; for those that remain the responsibility is mine. The reading-room staff of the Taylorian and Bodleian Libraries have on all occasions been courteously helpful and efficient in procuring the books I needed there. To my family, most of them happily unaware of Perrault except through the good offices of Walt Disney, I am grateful for giving me much to think about as regards children and parents. A good deal of the introduction derives ultimately from that source. To my sister Veronica I am grateful, among other things, for some precious insights into modern professional storytelling. To friends I am indebted for various things: for showing how it might be done, to Geoffrey Strachan; for help on spinning, to Janet Biggs; on Bettelheim, to Anne Hackmann; on medieval texts, to Linda Paterson; on door-latches, to Dave Roberts. To my wife Ann this book owes more than it would be possible to say. To her, after so many years, it is dedicated; without her it would not have been published.

# SELECT BIBLIOGRAPHY

❧❧

AMONG the items listed below, I have relied most heavily on the editions by Collinet and Rouger, on the catalogue of French tales by Paul Delarue and Marie-Louise Tenèze, and on the works by the Opies and Marina Warner, which together would form the best introduction currently available to fairy-tale in general.

### Works by Perrault and his contemporaries

*Perrault's Tales of Mother Goose*, ed. Jacques Barchilon, 2 vols. (New York: Pierpont Morgan Library, 1956); i. edited text of the manuscript, with introduction on the tales, ii. facsimile of the 1695 manuscript of the first five prose tales.

*Contes de Perrault, facsimilé de l'édition originale de 1695–97*, photographic reprint with Preface by Jacques Barchilon (Geneva: Slatkine Reprints, 1980); contains the verse tales in the 1695 edition by J.-B. Coignard and the prose tales in the 1697 edition by Claude Barbin.

*Contes* (and other works), ed. Pierre Collinet (Paris: Gallimard, 1981).

*Contes*, ed. Gilbert Rouger (Paris: Garnier, 1967); includes Mlle Lhéritier, *Les Enchantements de l'éloquence*, and Mlle Bernard, *Riquet à la houppe*.

*Contes* (and other works), ed. Marc Soriano (Paris: Flammarion, 1989).

Charles Perrault, *L'Apologie des femmes* (Paris, 1694).

—— *Mémoires de ma vie* (Paris: Macula, 1993); photographic reprint of 1909 edition by Paul Bonnefon.

—— *Œuvres complètes*, ed. Marc Soriano (Paris: Flammarion, 1969–70).

Madame d'Aulnoy, *Contes des fées*, ed. Nadine Jasmin (Paris: Champion, 2004).

Mademoiselle Lhéritier, Mademoiselle Bernard, and others, *Contes*, ed. Raymonde Robert (Paris: Champion, 2005).

### Reference Works

Delarue, Paul, and Marie-Louise Tenèze, *Le Conte populaire français, catalogue raisonné . . .*, 5 vols. (Paris: various publishers, 1957–2004).

Thompson, Stith, *Motif-Index of Folk Literature: A Classification of Narrative Elements*, rev. ed., 6 vols. (Bloomington: Indiana University Press; Copenhagen: Rosenkilde & Bagger, 1955–8).

Uther, Hans-Jörg, *The Types of International Folktales: A Classification and Bibliography based on the System of Antti Aarne and Stith Thompson*, 3 vols. (Helsinki: Academia Scientiarum Fennica, 2004); supersedes Aarne–Thompson, *The Types of the Folktale*.

Zipes, Jack, *The Oxford Companion to Fairy Tales* (Oxford, 2000).

### Works concerning Perrault and fairy-tale

Barchilon, Jacques, *Le Conte merveilleux français de 1690 à 1790* (Paris: Champion, 1975).

—— and Peter Flinders, *Charles Perrault* (Boston: Twayne, 1981); in English.

Bettelheim, Bruno, *The Uses of Enchantment: The Meaning and Importance of Fairy Tales* (New York: Knopf, 1976).

Cox, Marian Roalfe, *Cinderella: 345 Variants of Cinderella, Catskin, and Cap o' Rushes, abstracted and tabulated* (London: Folklore Society, 1893).

Dundes, Alan, *Cinderella: A Folklore Casebook*, 2nd edn. (Madison: University of Wisconsin, 1988).

——*Little Red Riding Hood: A Casebook* (Madison: University of Wisconsin, 1989).

Gélinas, Gérard, *Enquête sur les Contes de Perrault* (Paris: Imago, 2004).

Lüthi, Max, *Once Upon a Time: On the Nature of Fairy Tales* (Bloomington: Indiana University Press, 1970).

Marin, Louis, trans. Mette Hjort, *Food for Thought* (Baltimore: Johns Hopkins University Press, 1987).

Opie, Iona and Peter, *The Classic Fairy Tales* (Oxford: Oxford University Press, 1974).

Philip, Neil, *The Cinderella Story. The Origins and Variations of the Story known as 'Cinderella'* (Harmondsworth: Penguin, 1989).

Robert, Raymonde, *Le Conte de fées littéraire en France de la fin du XVIIème à la fin du XVIIIème* (Nancy: Presses universitaires, 1981).

Seifert, Lewis C., *Fairy Tales, Sexuality, and Gender in France, 1690–1715: Nostalgic Utopias* (Cambridge: Cambridge University Press, 1996).

Soriano, Marc, *Le Dossier Perrault* (Paris: Flammarion, 1972).

—— *Les Contes de Perrault, culture savante et traditions populaires*, rev. ed. (Paris: Gallimard, 1977).

Tatar, Maria, *Secrets Beyond the Door: The Story of Bluebeard* (Princeton: Princeton University Press, 2004).

—— (ed.), *The Classic Fairy Tales, Texts, Criticism* (New York: Norton, 1999).

Thompson, Stith, *The Folktale* (Berkeley and Los Angeles: University of California Press, 1977; first published 1946).

Warner, Marina, *From the Beast to the Blonde: On Fairy Tales and their Tellers* (London: Chatto & Windus, 1994).

—— (ed.), *Wonder Tales* (London: Chatto & Windus, 1994) (translated tales by Mme d'Aulnoy, Mlle Lhéritier, and others).

Zipes, Jack, *Fairy Tales and the Art of Subversion* (London: Heinemann, 1983).

—— *The Trials and Tribulations of Little Red Riding Hood*, 2nd rev. edn. (New York: Routledge, 1993).

### Websites

<www.pitt.edu/~dash/folktexts.html> (library of folk-tale, etc., edited by D. L. Ashliman), accessed 26 October 2008.

<www.surlalunefairytales.com> (texts of fairy-tales etc., edited by Heidi Anne Heiner), accessed 26 October 2008.

### Further Reading in Oxford World's Classics

Grimm, Jacob and Wilhelm, *Selected Tales*, trans. Joyce Crick.

# A CHRONOLOGY OF
# CHARLES PERRAULT

❧❧

1628  12 January: Charles Perrault born in Paris, son of Pierre Perrault and Pâquette Leclerc. He is one of twin boys; the other survives only a few months. The elder brother Pierre acts as godfather.

c.1643  Abandons school and with a friend, Beaurain, continues his education separately.

Death of Louis XIII; the 4-year-old Louis XIV succeeds him, with his mother Anne of Austria as Regent. The Chief Minister is Mazarin.

1648–53  The Fronde, the name given to prolonged civil conflicts between the royal or Court party, led by Anne of Austria and Mazarin, and the party of the Parlements (the highest law-courts, with important political rights) and some elements of the nobility. It ends in victory for the Court.

1651  Perrault gains the legal qualifications required to plead in a court of law, but does so only twice.

1652  His father dies.

1653  First published work, written in conjunction with his brothers and Beaurain.

1654  His brother Pierre buys a position as tax official, and employs him as clerk.

1657  His mother dies.

1659  Treaty of Pyrenees puts an end, for the time being, to war between France and Spain. A result is the marriage in 1660 of Louis XIV to Maria Theresa of Spain; Perrault writes an ode on the subject which finds favour with Mazarin.

1661  Death of Mazarin. Louis takes power personally, replacing Fouquet, the Minister of Finance, later convicted on corruption charges, with Colbert.

1663  Perrault is asked to write a poem on the sale of Dunkirk to France by Charles II, in 1662, as evidence of his ability to be a member of a committee, the 'petite académie', which is to advise Colbert on aspects of the cultural policy of glorifying the achievements of

Louis XIV's reign; he is successful and becomes secretary of the committee.

1665 He is appointed First Commissioner of Royal Buildings; in 1667 he becomes secretary of a committee, also including his architect brother Claude, advising on the design of the Louvre.

1666 Louvois becomes minister of war.

1671 Perrault becomes a member of the French Academy, having recently published a poem on the 'Carrousel de 1662', a spectacular royal equestrian show.

1672 1 May: he marries Marie Guichon.

He is elected Chancellor of the Academy (and re-elected next year, a special distinction), and begins a programme of reforms of Academy procedures, some designed to hasten work on its long-delayed Dictionary.

He is appointed General Controller of Buildings, a position created for him by Colbert.

France in alliance with England declares war on Holland.

1675 He publishes a *Recueil de divers ouvrages* ('Collected works of various kinds'), many written in honour of Louis XIV and his achievements.

25 May: his first son is baptized. (This normally occurred within a day or two of birth.)

1676 20 October: a second son is baptized.

1678 21 March: a third son, Pierre, later known as Pierre Darmancour, is baptized.

October: Marie Guichon dies.

Treaty of Nijmegen ends war against Holland.

1680 Perrault's duties as first commissioner are taken over by Colbert's son.

1681 He ceases almost completely to work for Colbert, and becomes Director of the French Academy.

Beginning of 'dragonnades', persecution of Huguenots when soldiers are billeted on them by Louvois.

1683 Perrault signs last documents as controller of buildings. Colbert dies, and Louvois takes over his ministerial duties; Perrault is excluded from his position.

Death of Maria Theresa. Probable date of morganatic marriage of Louis to Mme de Maintenon.

1685 Revocation of Edict of Nantes, which in 1598 had ensured Huguenots' religious and civil rights; they leave France in large numbers.

Enforced conversion of others to Catholicism; Perrault publishes an ode to the new converts.

1686  He publishes his poem *Saint Paulin*, dedicated to the leading church-man of the time, Bossuet, and much derided later by Boileau.

1687  His poem *Le Siècle de Louis le Grand* ('The Century of Louis the Great') is read at the Academy, which marks a new beginning for the Quarrel of the Ancients and the Moderns.

1688  He publishes the first volume of his *Parallèle des anciens et des modernes*, comparing ancient and modern achievements in numerous fields; three further volumes will appear, in 1690, 1696, and 1697.

War of League of Augsburg begins, France against Spain and northern powers; in 1689 England and Holland join the League to form the Grand Alliance, intended to prevent further French expansion.

1691  *Griselda* ('*La Marquise de Salusses ou La Patience de Griselidis*') is read at the Academy; it appears in the Proceedings of the Academy for the year, and is also published separately.

1693  Controversy with Boileau over the Ancients and the Moderns continues with hostile publications on both sides.

November: *Three Silly Wishes* ('*Les Souhaits ridicules*') appears in the *Mercure galant*.

1694  The three verse tales, *Griselidis*, *Peau d'Ane*, and *Les Souhaits ridicules*, are published together.

Perrault publishes his *Apologie des femmes* ('A Defence of Women') in response to Boileau's tenth Satire, an attack on women and marriage.

A serious famine occurs, followed by drought; Perrault publishes an ode to St Geneviève, the patron saint of Paris, believed to have brought relief to the city.

1695  Publication of an edition of the tales in verse containing the Preface for the first time.

Presentation manuscript, written by a scribe, of five prose tales (*Sleeping Beauty*, *Red Riding-Hood*, *Bluebeard*, *Puss in Boots*, *The Fairies*), dedicated to 'Mademoiselle', Elisabeth-Charlotte d'Orléans, the King's niece. The dedicatory epistle is signed 'P.P.' (Pierre Perrault).

October: Perrault's relative Mlle Lhéritier publishes her *Œuvres mêlées* ('Miscellaneous Works'), including *Marmoisan*, which she dedicates to Perrault d'Armancour's sister (the only known reference to her existence), and *Les Enchantements de l'Eloquence*, a tale very similar to Perrault's *The Fairies*.

1696 *Sleeping Beauty* is published separately in the *Mercure galant*.

May: Catherine Bernard publishes her novel *Inès de Cordoue*, which contains her own story of *Riquet à la houppe*.

October: *privilège* (licence to publish) a volume entitled *Récits ou Contes du temps passé* ('Stories or Tales of Bygone Times'), originally granted to the 'sieur P. Darmancour', Charles's son Pierre, is ceded to the publisher Barbin.

1696 or early 1697  Mme d'Aulnoy publishes her first three volumes of *Contes des fées*.

1697 Perrault's eight prose tales are published by Barbin under the definitive title *Histoires ou Contes du temps passé. Avec des moralités* ('Stories or Tales of Bygone Times, with Morals'), and with a frontispiece showing an old woman telling tales to children, under a scroll with the words 'Contes de ma mère l'oye' ('Tales of Mother Goose').

April: a younger neighbour of Pierre Perrault's dies, having been wounded by him in a sword-fight. Charles, legally responsible while his son is a minor, is sentenced to pay damages to the neighbour's mother, and again in April 1698.

Treaty of Ryswick ends War of League of Augsburg with losses of territory gained by France since 1688.

1699 Perrault publishes a translation of fables by Gabriele Faerno.

1700 March: death of Pierre, by now a soldier in one of the royal regiments.

1703 May: death of Charles.

# TALES IN VERSE

# Preface

꙳Ꙭ꙳

THE manner in which the public has received the pieces in this collection when each has been published separately* has given me a degree of confidence that they will not fail to please when appearing together. It is true that certain people who affect an air of gravity, and have enough understanding to see that these tales are intended for entertainment and contain nothing of high importance, have looked upon them with contempt; but it has been satisfactory to see that people of taste have not been of the same opinion. They have observed with pleasure that these tales, trifles though they are, are not only that, but carry a useful message; the diverting narrative is but an outer covering, chosen merely in order that they should be grasped more easily by the mind, and thus be agreeable and instructive at the same time.

That should have been enough for me not to fear any reproach that I have been spending my time on frivolous pursuits. However, since I have to deal with people who will not be contented with reason alone,* but can only be influenced by the authority of the Ancients and the examples which they have set, I will give them satisfaction in that regard also.

The Milesian Tales* which were so well-known among the Greeks, and afforded great delight to the Athenians and Romans, were no different in kind from the tales in this collection. The tale of the Widow of Ephesus* is of the same nature as *Griselda*: both are short stories, that is to say, narratives of events which could have happened, and which contain nothing absolutely contrary to probability. The fable of Psyche, as told by Lucian and Apuleius,* is pure fiction, an old wives' tale like that of Donkey-Skin. Thus in Apuleius it is recounted by an old woman

to a girl who has been abducted by robbers, just as the tale of
Donkey-Skin is told to children, day in day out, by their governesses and grandmothers. The fable of the ploughman* who
obtained from Jupiter the power to bring sunshine or rain as he
pleased, and who having used his power harvested nothing but
straw, and no crops of grain, because he had failed to request
any wind, or cold, or snow or any other kind of weather, such as
is necessary to make plants produce their seeds—this fable, I
observe, is of the same kind as the tale of the Three Silly Wishes,
except that one is serious and the other comic; but the lesson of
both is that men do not know what they need, and do better if
they let themselves be governed by Providence than if they
could make everything happen as they chose.

Having such fine models to follow from the wisest and most
learned writers of antiquity, I do not see that anyone has the
right to criticize me in this respect. I would even claim that my
fables are worthier of being retold than the majority of ancient
tales, especially those about the Widow of Ephesus and Psyche,
when they are regarded from the point of view of morality,
which is the main consideration in any kind of fable, and must
be the reason why they were invented. The only moral lesson to
be drawn from *The Widow of Ephesus* is that often those women
who seem the most virtuous are the least so, and consequently
that there are almost no truly virtuous women. Anyone can see
that this morality is very bad, and tends only to corrupt women
by giving them a bad example, making them believe that if they
fail in their duty they are merely doing the same as the majority.
It is different with the moral of *Griselda*, which encourages them
to put up with the behaviour of their husbands, and seeks to
show that there is no husband so brutal and capricious that,
through her patience, an upright woman cannot change his
character.

As regards the fable of Psyche, which in itself is delightful,
and very ingenious, I will compare the moral concealed in it to

that of *Donkey-Skin* when I have discovered what it is; but hitherto I have been unable to guess. I know that 'psyche' means the soul; but I cannot grasp what we are supposed to understand by Love* being in love with Psyche, that is, with the soul, and I can grasp even less the additional idea that she would have been happy as long as she did not know who her lover was, that is, Love, but that as soon as she knew she would become very unhappy. For me, such obscurity is impenetrable. The only comment I can make is that this fable, like the majority of the myths which have come down to us from antiquity, was invented for the sake of entertainment, with no regard to morality, which their authors seriously neglected.

The situation is different with the stories which our ancestors made up for the benefit of their children. They did not narrate them with the elegance and the embellishments with which the Greeks and Romans enhanced their fables, but were very careful to see that their tales contained instructive and commendable moral lessons. In every case virtue is rewarded and vice punished. Every story tends to show how advantageous it is to be honest, patient, careful, industrious, and obedient, and if not, the harm that will ensue. Here you find a fairy who makes a gift to a girl who answers her politely, which is that every word she speaks will turn to a diamond or pearl in her mouth; and to another girl who replies coarsely another gift, that the words in her mouth will turn into frogs and toads. Elsewhere there are children who, having duly obeyed their father or mother, become great lords, or who having been bad and disobedient fall into the most dreadful misfortune.*

However fanciful or extraordinary the events in all these fables may be, there can be no doubt that they instil in children both the desire to resemble the characters who are seen to become happy, and fear of the disasters which befall those characters who are wicked. And is it not a matter for praise if, when children are not yet of an age to see the value of sound moral

truths presented to them without adornment, their mothers and
fathers should make them appreciate these truths, and if I may
so express it, swallow them, by wrapping them up in stories
which are entertaining and appropriate to their tender years? It
is incredible how eagerly these innocent souls, in whom natural
rectitude has not yet been corrupted, absorb these disguised lessons; you see them despondent and miserable when the hero or
heroine of the tale suffers misfortune, and cry out for joy when
the time comes for them to be happy; and similarly, having
found it hard to bear when a wicked man or woman prospers,
they are delighted to see them punished at last as they deserve.
Thus seeds are sown which at first produce only the emotions of
joy or sadness, but scarcely ever fail to bring forth a propensity
for good.

I might have given my tales wider appeal if I had taken some
liberties and included some things of the kind that are customar-
ily employed to add humour;* but the desire to please the public
has never tempted me sufficiently to break a self-imposed rule
not to write anything that could be injurious to decency and
propriety.

Touching this point, I append a few lines of verse composed
by a young lady of much intelligence,* who wrote them out at
the end of *Donkey-Skin*, which I had sent her.

> The tale of Donkey-Skin is here retold
> So vividly, with such finesse,
> That my enjoyment was no less
> Than when by firelight Gran or nurse would hold
> My infant mind entranced as by a spell.
> We see some shafts of satire here as well,
> But free from any bitterness or spite;
> Thus all may read the story with delight.
> Besides, it is agreeable to find
> A simple, charming tale of such a kind

That while its lines amuse and entertain,
Our husbands, priests and mothers do not need
To criticize in case they might contain
Some things that wives and children should not read.

# The History of Griselda*

❧

TO MADEMOISELLE . . .*

*I here portray, to put before the eyes*
*Of one both beautiful and young, but wise,*
*Heroic patience: not, I ought to say,*
*For you to imitate in every way—*
*That's something which I don't presume to ask;*
*It really is too great a task.*
*In Paris, though, where men are civilized,*
*The sex created to arouse desire*
*Is given all it might require,*
*And every pleasure that can be devised.*
*But bad examples everywhere abound;*
*They are pernicious; better not neglect*
*Whatever method can be found*
*To counter them and weaken their effect.*
*With this in mind I honour as I should*
*A woman truly patient, truly good:*
*Her like, although surprising anywhere,*
*Would surely be a marvel here.*
*For in this happy climate, women seem*
*To rule us: everything is done*
*To suit their wishes, and each one*
*Acts like a queen and reigns supreme.*
*In Paris, then, I fear Griselda's fate*
*Is most unlikely to provoke*
*Much interest: it will merely seem a joke,*
*Her virtues quaint, her patience out of date.*
*It isn't that these virtues are unknown*
*To Paris ladies—no, indeed;*
*For as we have consistently been shown*
*Patience is what their husbands need.*

WHERE under Alpine heights\* the river Po
    Escapes from reed-filled pools to flow,
A little stream at first, and then to glide
Deeper and fuller through the countryside,
A young prince lived, a valiant lord
Whom all his provinces adored;
In his creation Heaven showed
That sometimes it combines in one
Those gifts more commonly bestowed
Singly upon some favoured son—
Rare qualities it only brings
To make the very greatest kings.

This Prince, then, marvellously blessed
With talents both of body and of soul,
Was strong and dextrous, fit to play the role
Of Mars in war; but also he possessed
That sacred flame, an instinct of the heart
Which made him cherish all the forms of art.
Brave deeds he loved, and daring enterprise,
Loved combat too, and victory in war—
Whatever brings renown, and glorifies
A noble name. He valued even more,
Generous as he was by temperament,
The lasting glory that a prince obtains
When everywhere in his domains
The people's lives are happy and content.

But on this noble nature shadows lay:
To dark and angry moods his soul fell prey,
And in his heart he steadfastly believed
That every woman constantly deceived.

The worthiest among them were, he thought,
Mere hypocrites who always sought,
Like enemies both proud and cruel,
Concealing their intent, to subjugate
The men who by unlucky fate
Were yielded up for wives to rule.
He saw around him husbands tamed,
Or even worse, betrayed and shamed,
A sight which fed his hatred even more,
As did the jealous habits of those climes;
And as a consequence he swore,
Not only once, but many times,
That if a kindly heaven were to make
A new Lucretia solely for his sake,
He'd still refuse, without debate,
To be imprisoned in the married state.

Each day, the morning was the time he spent
On government, deciding what was best
To keep his people settled and content.
To orphaned children, widows dispossessed,
He offered help, and saw their wrongs redressed;
Or else might seek to abrogate
A needless tax now out of date,
Devised and levied long before
To finance some unwanted war.

With business over, hunting took its place
Throughout the afternoon: he loved the chase;
Despite their rage, the boar and savage bear
Provoked in him much less alarm
Than women's soft beguiling charm;
He shunned their presence everywhere.
Meanwhile his subjects have in mind

Some other interests: their own.
For when another ruler mounts the throne
They want to see him temperate and kind,
Just like their Prince; and often urge their lord
To get a son, ensuring his succession.
One day, to plead their case, with one accord
They visited the palace in procession.
An orator, considered then the best,
Whose gravity of manner much impressed,
Said all he could in such a situation.
He emphasized with fervour their desire
To see the Prince well married, and the sire
Of generation after generation
Forever bringing riches to the nation.
And finally his tone rose even higher:
He saw a starry vision in the skies;
Among the offspring from the marriage bed
A glorious crusader would arise
Whose deeds would fill the heathen Turk with dread.

With plainer words, his voice less loud,
The Prince in answer thus addressed the crowd:
'I have been glad today to see your zeal
In urging me to seek a bride:
I thank you, and am gratified
To see the love and loyalty you feel.
It is my wish to do my best
To undertake at once what you suggest.
Choosing a wife, however, to my mind,
For most men is a difficult affair;
The more they try to take the proper care,
The greater are the problems that they find.
Young women, as you will observe,
While in the family home preserve

Such virtues as sincerity,
Decorum, helpfulness and modesty;
But once they take the marriage vow,
Their future is secure, and now,
With no more need to masquerade,
Each one gives up the painful role she played,
And since she has a household of her own,
Is free at last to be herself alone.

'She of the gloomy sort, refusing fun,
Decides to be exceedingly devout;
She looks for things to make a fuss about,
And scolds us constantly; another one
Becomes a fully fledged coquette
With all the would-be lovers she can get,
But only chats and gossips all the time;
Another ardently takes part
In keen debates on books and art,
Lays down the law on prose and rhyme,
And tells our authors where they err;
She thinks she is a connoisseur.
Another takes to cards and dice,
And loses thousands in a trice;
Her rarest and most precious things,
Her brooches, necklaces, and rings,
All she possesses disappears,
Even the garments that she wears.

'Among the choices they have made
There's one point where it seems to me
That all of them, bar none, agree:
It's that they wish to be obeyed.
What I myself am certain of is this:
For there to be a chance of married bliss,

Authority must not be shared by both.
If therefore what you want to see
Is that I take the marriage oath,
Find me a woman who has never shown
The slightest disobedience: she must be
Of proven patience, modest, lacking pride,
And free from any wishes of her own.
When she is found, I'll take her for my bride.'

His speech is done: the Prince will not remain
A moment longer; leaping on his steed
He gallops off at breakneck speed
To join his huntsmen waiting on the plain.
Traversing grassy meads and fallow land
He finds his men at ease; as one, they stand,
Alert, to blow their horns, and all around
The forest dwellers tremble at the sound.
Amidst the stubble fields the scattered pack
Of coursing dogs runs wildly to and fro;
The bloodhounds have arrived: they've found the track
Towards the quarry's stronghold; eyes aglow,
They try to drag along, with straining neck,
The sturdy handlers holding them in check.

The Prince, when told that all was now prepared,
A scent discovered, instantly declared
The hunt could now begin; for men and hounds
The quarry is fair game. The horn resounds,
And through the forest horses neighing,
And dogs in great excitement baying,
Bring noise and tumult which the echoes make
Still louder; all the woodlands shake;
The huntsmen and their hounds advance
Into the trees, towards the forest's heart.

The Prince, however, for his part,
Through destiny, or simple chance,
Quitted the hunt, and chose to ride
Without companions, by a hidden way,
Which as he galloped took him far astray,
Till silence fell; the din of hunting died.

The spot to which this strange adventure led,
Its glinting streams, its trees of darkest green,
Inspired the mind with solemn dread;
Around him in that sombre scene
So vividly did Nature's self appear,
So simply and so purely was she dressed,
That as he stood and gazed he blessed
The error which had brought him there.

He mused, and felt that reverence and awe
Which mighty landscapes, woods, and lakes impart;
But looking from that lonely place,
A woman's figure that he saw
Enthralled and held him, head and heart:
He'd never seen such beauty and such grace.
She was a shepherd maid; she sat beside
A little stream, her grazing sheep nearby,
And spun her wool: with agile hands she plied
The spindle that she watched with practised eye.
So fair she was, she could have pacified
The angriest of men. Her lips had stayed
As fresh as if she were a child;
Her skin, beneath the woodland shade,
As pale as lilies; and her eyes, made mild
By soft brown eyelashes, shone bright,
More blue and clear than Heaven's light.

The Prince, transfixed, without a sound,
Stirred by her beauty, for a moment stood
To look at her, still hidden in the wood:
But then he moved. She heard; and looking round
Caught sight of him; with great dismay
She saw herself observed. At once she flushed;
Across her cheek the burning crimson rushed;
From modesty, she turned her face away,
And from embarrassment, to him became
More lovely still. He thought she had, behind
The guileless veil of her attractive shame,
That sweet simplicity of mind,
That innocence, which womankind,
So he believed, could now no longer claim;
But which in her he saw unspoiled and pure.

With hesitation he drew near,
The prey of unaccustomed fear,
And timidly, his voice unsure,
As tongue-tied as the maid, he said
That all his huntsmen having gone ahead,
He'd missed the path they'd taken; could she say
If men and hounds had passed that way?
'My lord,' she answered, 'you alone
Have come along this solitary track,
But do not worry: I will guide you back
Towards a path which will be known,
I think, to you.' Said he: 'Now Heaven be blessed
For such good luck! I know these woods of old,
But till this moment had not guessed
What precious treasure they might hold.'

Then as upon the water's marshy brink
She saw him kneel with arms outstretched,

Seeking to quench his thirst and drink:
'My lord!' she cried, 'a moment, if you will,'
And for this new admirer ran and fetched,
Inside her modest house, a cup to fill
And offer him, with movements full of grace.
Seeing the pleasure on her face,
No agate vase, he thought, or crystal glass,
Though brilliantly adorned with gold,
Or deeply carved, or intricately scrolled,
Would ever have the beauty to surpass,
For him, with all its frivolous display,
The cup she gave him made of humble clay.

To find the way towards the town,
They traverse wooded, steep, and rocky ground,
Cut through by torrents tumbling down.
The Prince, meanwhile, is looking round
To map the way: the lover's cunning mind
Takes note of every turning they have passed,
And every mark and sign by which to find
The shepherdess's house again. At last
They reach a grove where tangled branches cast
Their cooling shadows. Here he can descry
His palace with its golden rooftops, high
And far away across the plain.

The Prince and shepherdess must part:
With heavy step he went, feeling the pain
Of love lodged deep within his heart.
While riding home, the tender thought
Of what had passed between them brought
Some solace, but the anguish was renewed
By next day's dawn. He stayed in sullen mood,
Listless and bored, till once again

He can rejoin his hounds and men,
But not to hunt: that pleasure he eschews;
For having lost his escort by a ruse,
He has the happiness of being free
To find the shepherdess; he wants to seek
His way alone. His landmarks every peak,
Each carefully remembered tree,
Directed by love's instinct as he rides,
He finds the way despite its twists and turns,
Until he finally discerns
The valley where her simple dwelling hides.

She and her father dwell alone, he learns.
Griselda is her name. They live
Their quiet life on what their sheep can give.
She spins herself the fleeces that they shear.
To merchants in the town she seldom goes;
The two alone make all the clothes they wear.
As he stays on, his admiration grows
For all her qualities of heart and mind;
The more he sees, the more he is aware
How many virtues are in her combined;
And if (he thinks) she seems so fair,
The reason for her beauty lies
Within her soul: the lively flame
Which animates her is the same
That shines and sparkles in her eyes.

So quickly to have made so just a choice
Delighted him: he could not but rejoice;
And to his council, summoned that same day,
He made his purpose known without delay:
'My councillors: the people's loyal plea
I hereby grant; I now agree

To take at last my marriage vows.
The lady whom I shall espouse
Will not be from some foreign land,
But from among you, near at hand;
In character, of proven worth;
Fair to behold; of honourable birth.
My forebears more than once have done the same.
But as for who she is, you must await
The day itself: until we celebrate
My wedding, I shall not disclose her name.'

Then instantly the tidings spread
Of everything the Prince had said;
The people's joy, as they received
The happy news, will scarcely be believed;
But of them all, the orator displayed
The deepest satisfaction: in his view
The credit for the public glee was due
Entirely to the moving speech he'd made;
A most important man he claimed to be.
'For eloquence has power to convince,'
He said each moment, 'even our great Prince.'

The ladies were a pleasant sight to see
As each, deluded, vainly tried
To tempt him as a suitor to her side;
For many times they'd heard their lord declare
That more than all things else he wished his bride
To charm him by her chaste and modest air.
In many ways their manners changed;
Their wardrobes too were rearranged.
When now they spoke their tones were soft,
Most piously they sniffed and coughed;
By half a yard coiffures descended,*

Of bosoms nothing was revealed,
While sleeves and cuffs were far extended
Till even fingers were concealed.

Meanwhile the wedding day approaches;
In every street and every square
Artists and artisans prepare
Superb new carriages and coaches,
So splendidly designed and made
That of the beauties there displayed
The least amazing to behold
Are rich adornments all of gold.
And so that nothing can obstruct
The view of the procession passing by
In all its splendour, labourers construct
Great stands on scaffolding built high;
Triumphal arches too they raise,
Which glorify the Prince, and praise
Not only all his victories in the field,
But his defeat, since Love has made him yield.

Others again, with diligence and skill,
Busily make those fiery toys, which fill
The air with harmless thunder, and release
New stars in myriads across the sky.
The ballet-dancers can be seen nearby,
At practice on their latest clever piece
Of pleasing nonsense, never seen before.
Opera too is in rehearsal here,
The finest ever known; its cast
Of deities are working at a score
Replete with melodies which charm the ear.
The famous wedding day arrives at last:
The early morning sky is bright and clear,

And scarcely has its golden blue
Been touched by dawn's vermilion hue,
Than ladies wake, and leap from bed;
Eager to watch, the people spread
Along the streets, where guards are sent
To keep clear passage and prevent
Disturbances among the crowd.
Inside the palace, every room is loud
With flutes and bugles and the rustic sound
Of shawms and bagpipes, while outside you hear
The din of drums and trumpets all around.

And when the Prince and all his court appear
He's greeted with prolonged and joyous cries;
But then he causes much surprise:
He leaves the road and makes his way,
As was his habit every day,
Towards the forest. 'There you are,' they said;
Our Prince is acting in his usual fashion;
In love he may be, but his strongest passion
Is hunting still.' The Prince goes on ahead
Quickly across the meadows of the plain;
Amazing his companions once again,
He turns towards the hills and rides apace
By woodland tracks, delighted as before
To trace the winding path towards the door
Of his beloved's rustic dwelling-place.

Meanwhile Griselda knew no more
Than what she'd heard from common talk
About the wedding; so she meant,
Wishing to see this splendid sight, to walk
Towards the town and watch the great event.
Just on the point of leaving, she had dressed,
To honour the occasion, in her Sunday best.

'So early and so quickly on your way!'
With tender look, the Prince approaching said;
'No need, sweet shepherdess, to hasten so;
The wedding that you are to see today,
At which it is your Prince who is to wed,
Cannot be held unless you also go.
I love you; it is you I choose
Above a thousand others, young and fair,
To marry and to share with you my life,
Unless you tell me now that you refuse.'

'My lord,' she said, 'I scarcely dare
To hope to rise so far, and be your wife;
This is some jest of yours, at my expense.'
'Grisel,' he said, 'believe me: it is true;
Your father tells me he consents—
He was the only one who knew.
All that is needed now is that you deign,
Sweet shepherdess, to tell me you agree;
But you must also swear, for peace to reign
Eternally between yourself and me,
Henceforward to obey my will alone.'
'I swear,' she answered; 'I have always known,
Although the man I married might be poor,
That on all matters he would then decide,
And I obey with joy; how much the more
If you, my lord, should take me for your bride!'
Thus was the Prince's declaration made;
And while his courtiers, with a single voice,
Congratulate him on his choice,
The Prince prevails upon the shepherd maid
To go and change her country dress
For raiment more befitting a princess.
The ladies of the court best qualified

Are asked if they will help; inside
The tiny room their skill and care
Increase her elegance and grace
As each adornment finds its place.

The ladies have but one small room to share,
But much admire the house, so fresh and clean
That not a hint of poverty is seen,
And cool beneath a plane-tree's spreading shade
To them it seems a perfect place to dwell:
As if it came there by some magic spell.

Superbly and delightfully arrayed
Outside the little house the shepherdess
At length appears; her beauty and her dress
Bring long applause and praise; and yet
The Prince observes her splendour with regret,
Half-wishing that he could restore
The simple innocence she had before.
Meanwhile a coach and horses wait—
The coach of gold, with ivory inlaid.
Majestically, the shepherd maid
Steps in beside the Prince to ride in state.
He finds he has as great a cause for pride
In sitting there, Griselda at his side,
As if he led a victory parade
In which his martial trophies were displayed.
The courtiers all follow; they observe,
As they proceed, the rank that they deserve
Through lineage, or by their post at court.
Meanwhile in town few citizens remain:
Outside the walls, dispersed across the plain,
They know the Prince's purpose by report,
And patiently await their lord's approach.

He's seen: they run to meet him, and the coach
Can scarcely move, so dense becomes the crowd.
The joyful cries continue long and loud;
The horses grow alarmed, and struggle past,
With rearing heads and stamping feet,
Advancing less, it seems, than they retreat.

The couple reach the church at last,
And at the altar solemnize,
With vows that make eternal ties,
The union of two destinies combined.
Towards the palace then they make their way,
Where pleasures wait of every kind,
With jousting, tilting, dancing, games to play,
And merriment shared round on every side.
At dusk, the god of weddings is their guide:
They are by fair-haired Hymenaeus led
To the chaste delights of the marriage bed.

Next day came local worthies, small and great:
The nobles, church, and third estate
Sent delegations to express
Greetings to the Prince, and to the Princess.
Surrounded by the ladies of her court,
Without embarrassment of any sort,
Griselda listened as a princess should,
And answered as a princess would.
So skilfully did she perform her duty
That all could see how Heaven's treasure,
Reason and sense no less than beauty,
Had come to her in overflowing measure.

Thus gifted, she was quick to understand
The manners of the highest in the land

And make them hers; and soon became well-versed
In what her ladies each knew how to do,
And what they each enjoyed; so from the first,
With never-failing common sense, she knew
How they could be as easily controlled
As flocks of sheep when guided to their fold.

Within the year Heaven saw fit to bless
The marriage of this happy pair,
And though the child was not the son and heir
That both had wished for, yet the young princess
Had so much beauty that their one concern
Was to preserve her free from harm.
The Prince who found her sweet and full of charm
Would often visit, leave, but soon return;
Her mother would not have her out of sight,
But gazed on her with ever more delight.

For nourishment she thought it best
Herself to feed the baby at the breast:
'For how, without ingratitude,' she said,
'Could I refuse her, crying to be fed,
And leave that service to another
When I should give it? For what cause
Should I go contrary to nature's laws,
And be, to this dear child, but half a mother?'

Perhaps the Prince's love has ceased to blaze
As ardently as in its early days;
Or else some melancholic humour burns
Within him still, and now returns
In vapours rising once again
To make his heart corrupt and cloud his brain;
But now, in all she does, her acts appear,

To his imagination, insincere.
Her virtue irks him: in it he detects
A snare devised in order to deceive
His trusting soul; he thinks he should believe
All that his agitated mind suspects.
He had, it seemed, been happy to excess;
He now prefers to make himself unsure.

Disturbed in mind, he seeks a cure:
It pleases him to follow the Princess,
To spy upon her, and to make her bear
The torments of constraint, the pangs of fear,
And any method he can utilize
For truth to be distinguished from disguise.
'I've trusted her,' he thinks, 'too long;
And if her virtues should prove real,
The most unbearable ordeal
Will simply make them twice as strong.'

He keeps her in his palace, closely held,
The pleasures of the court now far away;
In isolation, she is forced to stay
Inside her room, whence daylight is expelled.
Convinced that ornament and proud display
Are what delight, above all things,
The sex that Nature made for beauty's sake,
He roughly says that he must take
Her pearls and rubies, jewels and rings,
Which he had given her to show
His tenderness a year ago.

For her, whose life is free from blame,
Duty has always been her only aim;
She gives the jewels back without distress,

And even, since to take them from her hands
Has pleased him, so she understands,
Her own contentment is no less
Than when she had them first as his Princess.

'These torments are for me,' she said, 'a test:
My husband makes me suffer in this way
To rouse my virtue, which too long a rest,
I know, would cause to perish and decay.
If such is not his plan, at least I'm sure
That what the Lord my God intends for me,
By such prolonged affliction, is to see
How far my constancy and faith endure.

'How many wretched women heed
Only their own desires; they go
By paths of danger, paths that lead
To empty pleasures, then to woe!
Meanwhile God's justice, sure and slow,
Allows them blindly to proceed;
Ignoring risk they do not shrink
Even upon the chasm's brink.
God treats me as a child whose need
Is to be guided and reproved;
Purely by goodness is he moved.
We ought to love the pains we bear:
To suffer brings us future joys;
We hold our Father's goodness dear;
So too the hands that he employs.'

Whatever the tyrannic Prince may ask
Is done at once. 'Her virtue is a mask,'
He thinks; 'which will no longer fool my eyes:
I now see through her long-maintained disguise.

My blows have failed in their effect
Because among the targets I select
There's nothing that she deeply cares about.
But yet she loves the young princess, no doubt;
There's nothing that is closer to her heart.
In her ordeal, the child must play its part.
Her daughter is the instrument I need
In order for my project to succeed.'

The babe beloved so deeply by her mother
Had just been at her breast, and lay,
Held tenderly to let her play,
Laughing as they gazed at one another.
'You love your daughter, I can see,' he said,
'But she is young, and it is my desire
To move her in good time, lest she acquire,
From you, manners which make her seem ill-bred.
Her education must be sound;
And now, by fortune's favour, I have found
A lady of distinguished mind
To teach her what a princess ought to be:
Of highest virtue, gracious, and refined.
I therefore hope you will agree
That she must go. Later today
Someone will come to take the child away.'
He left her then, not wishing to remain;
His heart was not so inhumane,
His eyes so cruel, as to stay
And see her parted from their love's one token,
The union of child and mother broken.

The tears ran freely down as the Princess
Sat with the child, in unrelieved distress;
Until the moment of her fate
She could do nothing else but wait.

When to the door the hated minion came
With cruel orders in his master's name,
She only said: 'I must not disobey,'
And gazing on the infant where she lay,
Took her, and with maternal ardour pressed
Her daughter for a moment to her breast,
While little arms returned a soft embrace,
And then, the tears still covering her face,
Gave up the child. Can pain be more severe?
For one who loved as tenderly as she,
To have the heart cut from her would not be
Worse than to lose the child she held so dear.

An old religious house, of much renown,
Stood at some little distance from the town,
Its virgins governed by austerity,
Its prioress revered for piety.
The child, along with jewels of great worth,
Was secretly brought here. About her birth,
Nothing was said; the convent, in due course,
Would be rewarded, so it was implied,
For all the care the sisters would provide.

Meanwhile the Prince was stricken by remorse,
And tried by going hunting to suppress
Thoughts of his cruelty to the Princess,
Whom he avoided, as one might avoid
A tigress when her cub has been destroyed.
He was astonished, when they met, to find
Her manner still affectionate and kind;
She had with him the same caressing ways
As in more fortunate and joyous days.

Such promptness to forgive renewed
The shame he felt for doing wrong,

But soon his black and hostile mood,
Despite his guilt, proved once again too strong;
He went to her, before two days had passed,
Making her torment worse, but feigning grief,
And said, their daughter's life had been too brief;
The child so dearly loved had breathed her last.

She staggered at this second mortal blow,
But saw the pallor of his face, and chose,
Putting her own despair aside,
With wifely love to soothe him, and provide
Some comfort for his simulated woes.
Such deep devotion on her part,
Such magnanimity, defied
The impulse to be harsh; it touched his heart
And changed him, almost making him confess
That death, in truth, had spared the young princess.
But then the better motive failed,
While spite and stubbornness prevailed,
And in the end the Prince did not reveal
A secret it was useful to conceal.

The sun, while fifteen years passed by,
Traversed his dozen mansions in the sky
To bring about the seasons' change,
But witnessed nothing that might disarrange
The wife's and husband's constant peace;
Unless to please himself, by sheer caprice,
He might provoke in her some discontent,
Intending only to prevent
The flames of love from burning low—
As when the smith, his task not yet complete,
Seeing his furnace dull and slow,
Upon the fading coals will throw
A splash of water to restore their heat.

And all this while the young Princess
Was growing up in years; she grew no less
In sense and virtue; to the graceful air,
The natural sweetness, from her mother's side,
She added all the dignity and pride
Which were her noble father's share.
The best of both her parents was combined
To make a beauty of the purest kind;
Wherever she was walking by
She seemed to bring some radiance from the sky.
One day a courtier, as it chanced,
Well born and young, the handsomest of men,
When visiting, caught sight of her: entranced,
He lost his heart and loved her there and then.

Now on the fairer sex Nature bestows
An instinct that the fairest all possess:
For when her eyes wreak havoc, each one knows
What injuries she causes, and can guess
How deep the unseen damage goes;
That she was tenderly adored
Was by the young Princess not long ignored.

Observing the proprieties, she tried
To overcome her feelings; not for long:
She yielded to them soon, for on her side
The love she felt for him was just as strong.
Her lover to his courtship brought
Great qualities: he was of high descent,
Good-looking, brave. For years, the Prince had thought
That if the young man ever sought
To be his son-in-law, he would consent.

It therefore pleased him when he learned
About this love that she returned;

But then a strange idea took hold: the pair,
Before he would allow them to secure
The happiness they longed to share,
Must have great torments to endure.
'I want these two to be content,' he said;
'But yet, in order for their love to grow
More firm and constant, they must undergo
A harsh ordeal of fear and dread.

'And at the same time I shall test
Griselda's patience once again;
But not because I still maintain
My wild suspicions: they are laid to rest;
No longer do I doubt her love; my aim
Is now to celebrate her worth;
How good and wise she is I shall proclaim;
Adorned by gifts so great, the earth,
In reverence and awe, will raise
A hymn of gratitude and praise.'

He chose in public to declare
That rashly married, and without an heir
To rule his land and people in due course,
His infant daughter also having died,
He had, to save his line, but one resource:
To find himself a second bride.
The high-born maid whom now he would espouse
Had led an innocent and cloistered life,
And soon, between them, marriage vows
Would crown his love by making her his wife.

I leave aside the torment and despair
Brought by these tidings to the youthful pair;
The Prince meanwhile informed his faithful spouse,

With neither tears nor anger in his eyes,
That they must part, and she must leave his house,
For fear of worse to follow otherwise.
She has his people's sentiments to thank:
They are indignant at her lowly rank,
And he must seek a bride of nobler stock.

'But as for you,' he said, 'you must return
Beneath your roof of thatch and fern,
And take your shepherdess's smock,
Laid ready for you in your room.'

She listened calmly as she heard her doom,
And did not flinch, nor did she speak;
She sought to keep her misery unseen;
Her countenance remained serene
Even as tears ran down her cheek,
And through the sorrow on her face
She kept her beauty and her grace,
As when the year brings spring again,
Its sunshine bright despite the rain.

She answered nearly fainting, with a sigh:
'My husband, lord and master: my reply,
Though nothing could be worse than what you say,
Will be to demonstrate to you
That all I ever wish is to obey.'
Then peacefully, and saying nothing more,
Secluded in her room where she withdrew,
She put away the costly clothes she wore,
And weeping inwardly took up the smock
Worn long ago to tend her flock.

Thus modestly and humbly dressed
She sought the Prince to make a last request:

'I am unable, Sir, to leave
Unless, having displeased you, I receive
Your pardon. Poverty I can endure,
But not your wrath. In truth, I do repent;
Grant me forgiveness, and, though poor,
I nonetheless shall live content,
And never will the years affect
My love for you, nor my respect.'

Dressed in her peasant clothes, she spoke
With such docility of mind,
In words so noble and refined,
That all his passion reawoke,
And almost led him to revoke
Her banishment; swayed by her charms,
And hardly able to suppress a tear,
He went towards her, drawing near
As if to take her in his arms,
But then his pride, with all its force,
Bade him be firm, and not change course;
It overcame the love within his heart,
And speaking harshly he replied:
'The past is finished; I am satisfied
That you repent. Now go; you must depart.'

She and her father went without delay.
Like her, he had been given rustic dress,
And as she saw him weeping with distress
That such disgrace should strike inside a day,
She said: 'From palace splendour we are banned
Without regret; so let us leave the court
For shady woods set in a wilder land,
Where homes are of a humbler sort,
And life is innocent; there we shall find
More true repose, and greater peace of mind.'

By slow and weary ways they reached at last
Their lonely place of exile; there she took
Distaff and spindle, sitting by the brook
To spin where she was courted in the past.
There for the Prince, a dozen times each day,
Without complaint, serene, she went to pray
That he would prosper, given Heaven's aid,
His hopes succeed, his glory never fade;
No wife caressed and kissed could be
More fervent in her love than she.

This husband, whom she loves and misses still,
Has not forgotten his intent
Of testing her; a messenger is sent
To tell her that it is his will
That from her distant dwelling-place
She must return, and see him face to face.

As soon as she appeared, he said: 'Grisel,
In church tomorrow I shall take as bride
A young princess. She must be satisfied
With all I do, and all you do as well.
It is your utmost care that I require;
I want you to assist in my desire
To please the one I love; you know
How I am to be served, and what is due
In princely houses: nothing mean or low;
But everything must clearly show
A prince can be a lover too.
These rooms are hers; use all your skill
To decorate them; see that they are graced
By all that wealth can buy, and fill
Each one with elegance and taste.
Remember always that your rule must be
To demonstrate how dear she is to me.

'And that you may more willingly assume
The tasks your duties here demand,
I show you now the lady whom
You serve henceforth by my command.'

Like nascent dawn in eastern skies,
Lovely to see when night has cleared,
The Princess brought, as she appeared,
As fair a sight before their eyes.

Griselda, when the girl arrived,
Felt love surge through her; in her head
The memories of former days revived,
Of happier times; and to herself she said:
'Alas! my daughter, if she had survived,
Had Heaven listened to my prayers, might be
Perhaps as tall, and not less fair than she.'

Griselda's wish to show her love and care
Was so intense, that when the girl had gone,
She thus addressed the Prince, still unaware
That instinct was the force that urged her on:
'Permit me, Sir, to make a plea
In favour of the maiden you will wed,
For she was tenderly brought up, and bred
To live in luxury and splendour, free
From any cruelty; she could not bear
The trials you imposed on me:
She would not live through treatment so severe.

'Of lowly birth and poor, I was inured
To toil and hardship; married, I endured
All kinds of misery and pain;
It did not vex me, nor did I complain,

But she has never suffered grief or woe.
The slightest harshness that you show
Will kill her; angry words, a look, no more,
Would be to her a mortal blow.
Alas! Sir, treat her kindly, I implore.'

The answer she received was stern:
'Attend to matters that are your concern.
A simple shepherdess should not advise;
I need no lessons; it is not for you
To tell me what I should or should not do.'
Griselda, lowering her eyes,
Remained in silence and withdrew.

Then soon appear on every side
The wedding guests, from far and wide;
Into the splendid palace hall,
Directed by the Prince, they came.
Before he lit the nuptial flame
He spoke as follows to them all:
'Appearances are not to be believed:
False hopes excepted, by no other thing
Are we more readily deceived;
And those you see before you here will bring
Convincing proof. For anyone would guess,
Seeing my bride, so soon to be my wife,
And by her marriage then a great princess,
That she has all she might desire from life.
Yet nothing could be further from the truth.

'Consider next this martial youth:
Do not appearances suggest
That such a warrior, pursuing fame,
Must be content to be our wedding guest,

Since in our tournaments he has the chance,
Before us all, to prove himself the best,
Showing his skill with sword and lance?
Yet what he wants is not what you expect.

'As for Griselda, surely the effect
Of all her sufferings must be
Despair, and rage, and tears? But no:
She does not weep, from rancour she is free,
Nor does she let the least impatience show.

'And who would not believe, again,
That I must be the happiest of men,
Seeing the beauty of my bride?
But were the knot of marriage tied
How pitiable would be my state!
No prince has known so terrible a fate.'

The Prince went on: 'Although what you have heard
Will baffle you, a word will make it clear;
And though I speak of sorrows, that one word
Will also make them disappear.
Know first, then, that you do not understand
Why I have brought this beauteous maiden here:
You think I mean to marry; but in truth
She is my daughter, and her hand
I now bestow upon this noble youth,
Who loves her heart and soul; she feels the same.

'And furthermore I now proclaim
That I continue to be deeply moved
To see my wise and faithful wife display
Such constant patience; she has proved
Still loyal when unjustly sent away.

'I take her back; her place is now assured;
And I will seek, with every delight
That tender love can offer, to requite
The cruel treatment she endured
When jealousy had filled my mind with spite.
To see her slightest wishes gratified
Will be my purpose now, with greater zeal
Than when, suspecting her, I tried
To break her patience with her long ordeal.
If future ages celebrate her name
For never yielding to the trials she bore,
Her peerless virtue justifies the fame
By which she will be honoured evermore.'

As when the skies are leaden grey
Obscuring all the light of day,
And everywhere the threatening cloud
Warns that a storm is close at hand:
If winds should part this gloomy shroud,
And spreading far across the land
The rays of sunshine, clear and bright,
Make it once more a joyous sight;
So too those eyes cast down by sadness
Were lifted now in sudden gladness.

Her unknown father has been found,
The secret of her birth explained;
The young princess's joy is unconstrained:
She casts herself upon the ground
Before the Prince, and there she kneels
To hold him closely; he at last reveals
His tender love: he lifts her to her feet,
Embraces her, then takes her hand,
And goes with her across the hall to greet

Her mother, who from joy can scarcely stand;
The sudden rapture makes her senses numb.
And though her heart, so grievously beset
By constant woes, has never yet,
In years of misery, been overcome,
The burden of delight is now too great:
She seems to sink beneath its weight.
She reaches out in order to embrace
Her cherished daughter, whom by Heaven's grace
She has recovered after all these years,
But then can only weep with happy tears.

At this, the Prince said: 'In some other place
You will be able to express
The love you feel: but now, you need to dress
As noblewomen do; your rank has changed;
A wedding also has to be arranged.'

To church the loving pair are led, and there
That each will cherish each they swear,
And forging bonds that none can sever
Engage themselves to love for ever.
Then follows every sort of pleasure:
Music-making, games, and dances,
Jousts with riders breaking lances,
And sumptuous feasts consumed at leisure.

Towards Griselda all direct their gaze:
Her patience, long and sorely tried,
Is now at last admired and glorified.
Indulgent to their lord's capricious ways,
The people in their joy can even praise
That cruel test Griselda had to face:
Without it, we should not have seen,

They say, that virtue which has always been,
Though rare at any time or place,
An honour to her sex, but shown
In perfect form by her alone.

## Letter to M. . . .,* on sending him
### *The History of Griselda*

꿍얼꿍

Had I submitted to all the different opinions I have been given about the work which I am sending to you, nothing would have remained of it except a simple story, plain and bare; in which case I would have done better not to have anything to do with it, but to leave it as it is between its blue covers,* where it has lain for so many years.

I read it first to two friends of mine.

'Why spend so long,' said one of them, 'on the character of your hero? We have not the slightest need to know what he did in his council in the mornings, and even less how he amused himself during the afternoon. All that sort of thing ought to be left out.'

The other said: 'For my part, I wish you would remove the humorous reply he makes to the representatives of his people when they urge him to get married; such remarks are inappropriate for a dignified and responsible prince. And if you would permit me,' he went on, 'I would advise you also to suppress your long description of the hunt. What relevance does it have to the basic story? Believe me, such adornments are empty and pretentious, which weaken your poem rather than enriching it. The same applies,' he added, 'to the preparations made for the Prince's wedding; the whole passage is pointless and unnecessary. As for your ladies who lower their coiffures, cover their bosoms, and lengthen their sleeves, the humour is feeble, as it is with the orator who congratulates himself on his eloquence.'

'I would also ask you,' said the one who had spoken first, 'to remove the Christian reflections made by Griselda, when she says that God wishes to put her to the test; it's not the right place for a sermon. And I cannot put up with the callous way in which the Prince treats her—it makes me angry, and I would leave it out. I know it is part of the story, but that's no matter. I would also remove the episode of the young lord, which is only there so that the young princess can get married: it makes the tale too long.'

'But,' I said, 'the story would end badly without it.'

'All I can say is,' he answered, 'that I would remove it all the same.'

A few days later, I read the piece to two other friends, who said not a word about the passages I have just mentioned, but took me to task over a number of others. 'Far from complaining that your criticisms are too harsh,' I told them, 'I am sorry that they are not more severe; you have let me get away with innumerable passages that have been found to deserve the strictest censure.'

'And which are those?' they asked.

'I have been told,' I said, 'that the description of the Prince's character takes too long, and that nobody is interested in what he did in the morning, and even less in the afternoon.'

'Criticism like that,' they both said together, 'cannot have been meant seriously.'

'I am also criticized,' I went on, 'for the reply made by the Prince to those who are urging him to get married, which is said to be too humorous, and beneath the dignity of a responsible prince.'

'Really?' said one; 'and why is there a problem when a prince in Italy, where it is common to hear joking remarks made by the most dignified of people, and those of the highest position, makes jokes about women and marriage, seeing that he makes a point of being hostile to them, and when in any case they are constantly the object of mockery? However that may be, I must plead for mercy on behalf of the passage in question, and also the passages about the orator who thinks he has converted the Prince and the coiffures that are worn lower; for critics who dislike the Prince's humorous answer will probably show no quarter to these either.'

'Your guess is correct,' I said. 'But from another angle, those who want only to be entertained cannot bear Griselda's Christian reflections, when she says that it is God who wishes to test her. They say they are an irrelevant sermon.'

'Irrelevant?' the other one replied; 'not only do they suit the subject, but they are absolutely necessary. You needed to make your heroine's patience credible; and what other means did you have, except to make her regard her husband's cruel treatment of her as coming from the hand of God? If it were not for that, she would be taken for the stupidest woman there has ever been, which would certainly not make a good effect.'

'They also dislike,' I told them, 'the episode in which the young lord marries the young princess.'

'They are wrong,' he responded; 'since the work is a true poem, although you call it a story, it is necessary that nothing should be left incomplete when it ends. But if the young princess were to go back to her convent without being married, although she was expecting to be, neither she, nor the readers of your story, would be content.'

As a result of this discussion I decided to leave my work more or less as it had been when it was read in the Academy.* In a word, I took care to correct anything that had been proved to be bad in itself, but as regards the passages which, I found, had no other fault except that they were not to the taste of certain people who were perhaps a little too fussy, I left them as they were.

> I give a meal: a single guest
> Unfortunately dislikes one course;
> So must I then agree perforce
> To leave it out but keep the rest?
> 'Live and let live,' they say, is best;
> To satisfy our different wishes
> Menus must offer different dishes.

Whatever the truth of the matter, I thought that I should leave it to the public, whose decisions are always right. I shall learn from them what to think on the question, and I shall scrupulously follow their opinion if a second edition of this work should ever happen to be published.*

# Three Silly Wishes*

❧

TO MADEMOISELLE DE LA C.*

*You're sensible, I know, Mademoiselle;*
*If it were otherwise, I'd take good care*
*Never to let you read or hear*
*The comic tale I have to tell.*
*It's not romantic; it's about*
*A length of sausage. 'Oh, my dears!*
*How dreadful!' simpering girls cry out,*
*'For shame! a sausage? fie!'—for theirs*
*Are hearts more earnestly inclined;*
*Their books are of another kind:*
*They're full of tender love-affairs.*
*But, Mademoiselle, for you who are,*
*When telling tales, ahead by far*
*Of all the rest; you who beguile*
*Both eye and ear, making us seem to see,*
*Not merely hear the story, since your style*
*Is natural and vivid: you'll agree*
*That manner and not matter is the key;*
*For what we prize a story for*
*Is less what it's about, and more*
*The way it's told. If this is true,*
*I'm sure you'll like my tale; its moral too.*

A WOODCUTTER there was, once long ago,
Who, weary of the wretched life he led,
Had one desire: to rest in peace, he said,
Upon the shores of Acheron\* below
In Hades. This was his pitiable claim:
Whatever wish he'd made, since he was born,
The gods' response had always been the same:
They'd treated him with cruelty and scorn.

One day, as he complained, there in the wood
The great god Jupiter before him stood,
Complete with thunderbolt. The man's dismay
Was more than I can easily portray.
'I ask you nothing,' trembling, on his knees,
He said; 'No wish from me, oh lord, and please
No lightning, sir; and then we'll be all square.'
'Mortal,' said Jupiter, 'be not afraid;
I come, moved by the protests you have made,
To show you that your judgements are unfair.
Attend therefore. You are allowed to make
Three wishes; and, whatever they may be,
As master of the world I undertake
At once to grant them fully. On your side,
Think what will make you happiest, and see
How best your needs can now be satisfied.
Your happiness depends on how you use
This chance: reflect with care before you choose.'

The god, so saying, skywards took his flight.
The man heaved up his bundle on his back
And high in spirits took his homeward track;
His load of logs had never seemed so light.

Said he, while jogging cheerfully along:
'Now this is serious; the proper way
Is not to rush; we mustn't get it wrong;
I'll find out what the missus has to say.'
Arriving at the wretched hovel which
Served as his home, he cried: 'Hey, Meg! we're rich!
Let's have a feast tonight—stoke up the fire!
Just wish, that's all—we'll get what we desire!'
Then he explained in detail what had passed.
His spouse's mind was working fast,
And soon she readily devised
A hundred plans; but recognized
The pressing need for care and tact,
And said: 'Good William, we must act
Without impatience; too much haste,
And all our hopes could go to waste.
Together let's discuss what's best to do,
Then sleep on it. Tomorrow we shall see
Exactly what these wishes ought to be.'

Her William says: 'That's my opinion too.
Now Meg, some wine: go to the special cask—
You know—behind the logs, and fill a flask.'
On her return, he drinks, and takes his seat
To rest awhile beside the blaze.
And then: 'If only, by this fire,' he says,
I had a length of sausage here to eat;
My dearest wish, is that.' And as he speaks,
His wife perceives with much surprise
A sausage of imposing size
Approaching from the hearth. She shrieks;
But it continues its advance,
Wriggling towards her on the floor.
A moment's thought, and she is sure

That what has caused this strange mischance
Must be the careless wish her man
Has stupidly and rashly made.
Much mortified, she then began
An angry conjugal tirade.
Upon the wretched William's head
Were heaped reproaches and abuse.
'You could have been an emperor,' she said,
'With clothes of gorgeous silk, you silly goose,
And diamonds, rubies, pearls, and gold. Instead,
Sausage is what you choose, for Heaven's sake!'
'All right; I've chosen badly, I confess,'
He said, 'I made a serious mistake;
Next time I'll do better.' She said: 'Oh yes?
And pigs might fly. The man's a proper ass
Who'd wish for something so completely crass.'

Enraged, the husband more than once came near
To wishing that his Meg might disappear.
(Between ourselves, without this wife
He might have had a better life.)
'We men,' he cried, 'are born to constant woes.
Plague take the woman, and the sausage too!
I wish to God, you evil-tempered shrew,
That now it hung upon your nose!'
No sooner had he said this word
Than high in Heaven the wish was heard.
The sausage stuck; and by a yard or more
Meg's nose grew longer. She was cross before;
This latest unforeseen event
Did not reduce her discontent.
Meg was attractive; she'd a pretty face;
And speaking honestly, with due respect
For truth, this decoration, in that place,

Did not produce a good effect.
However, it compelled her, as it hung
Over her mouth and chin, to hold her tongue,
And since a husband naturally seeks
To have a wife who seldom speaks,
For him a silent wife was bliss;
He couldn't wish for more than this.

But then he thought, as inwardly he mused:
'This accident's a dreadful thing,
But with one wish remaining to be used
I could, all in one go, become a king.
A king!—with that, there's nothing can compare.
But what about the future queen?
She might be plunged in deep despair
As things are now, if she were seen
Upon her throne, in robes and crown,
With all that sausage hanging down.
On this, it's right to hear her views;
For she must be the one to choose
Whether she rather would, or not,
Be queen and keep the awful nose she's got,
Or else be what she was before,
A woodman's wife and nothing more,
But with a nose of normal size,
As it was once, till everything went wrong.'

Now even though there's no one who denies
That grandeur, rights, and powers belong
To kings and queens; though everybody tries
To praise a royal nose, however long;
Yet since what women yearn for most of all
Is to attract, she kept her peasant's shawl,
For that was what she finally preferred,

Rather than be a queen and look absurd.
The husband, too, remained a woodman still.
He didn't rule as emperor, or fill
His purse with golden coins. His last resource,
His one remaining wish, was used, of course,
As best he could: to see his wife once more
Looking the same as she had been before.

To wish aright is not for humankind:
We are too rash, improvident, and blind.
Whatever the gifts that Heaven may dispense,
Not many men will use them with good sense.

# Donkey-Skin

❧

TO THE MARQUISE DE LAMBERT*

*Some lofty persons seldom smile,*
*And cannot bear to give their time,*
*Regarding literary style,*
*To anything that's not sublime.*
*With views like theirs I can't agree.*
*The highest minds, it seems to me,*
*May sometimes condescend to go*
*To watch, let's say, a puppet-show,*
*Without incurring loss of face.*
*Given the proper time and place,*
*Sublimity may suit less well*
*Than some diverting bagatelle.*
*Nor should it cause us much surprise*
*That men of sense, at times oppressed*
*By hours of work, should think it wise*
*To free themselves from reason's bonds,*
*And pleasantly be lulled to rest*
*By some old tale of maids distressed,*
*Of ogres,* spells, and magic wands.*
*Ignoring, then, the blame I may incur*
*For wasting time, I'll do as you prefer,*
*Madame; so let me now begin*
*The tale, in full, of Donkey-Skin.*

There ruled a mighty king in days of yore,
Greater than any who had ruled before;
Well-loved in peace, in war arousing fear,
No other king could claim to be his peer.

With enemies subdued, his triumphs made
A shield for peaceful virtues, arts, and trade,
And brought prosperity in place of strife.
The charm and beauty of his faithful wife,
As gentle and as kind as she was fair,
Entranced him still: at home he had the air
Less of a king with consort at his side,
And more the bridegroom with his radiant bride.
The union of this loving pair
Produced no other child but one,
And that a daughter, not a son;
In virtue, though, beyond compare:
And so her parents did not much repine
That she alone would carry on their line.

Throughout the palace of this king
Magnificence was everything.
Footmen and courtiers by the score
Were swarming in each corridor;
Great stables had been built to hold
Each and every breed of horse,
In many sizes, all, of course,
Caparisoned in cloth of gold.
A truly striking sight was there:
The place of honour was reserved
For Donkey Ned with wagging ear.
You think this honour undeserved?
Then hear how justified it is
By Ned's amazing qualities.
Nature had made the beast so pure
That what he dropped was not manure,
But sovereigns and gold crowns instead
(Imprinted with the royal head)
Which every morning Master Ned
Left for collection on his bed.

But Heaven grows tired, now and then,
Of granting happiness to men,
And puts some sorrows in our way
Like rainstorms on a sunny day.
A sickness struck the King's beloved wife,
Grew worse and worse: it soon attacked her life.
Help was sought throughout the land,
Doctors arrived on every hand.
The Faculty of Medicine was consulted:
They looked in books by ancient Greeks,
While fashionable alternative techniques
Were counselled by the quacks: no cure resulted.
The patient worsened. Nothing could arrest
The malady which daily still progressed.

The Queen, then, feeling close to death,
Addressed, in solemn words, the King:
'Permit me with my dying breath
To ask of you, my dear, one thing:
That if you should desire to wed
When I am gone . . .' 'Alas!' her husband said,
'Have no anxieties of such a kind;
For never will I take another bride;
So please dismiss these worries from your mind.'
'That's what I thought you'd say, my dear,' replied
The Queen; 'of that your passion makes me sure;
But yet I'd like to feel still more secure:
I'd like to hear you swear an oath
(On which I know I can rely)
That only if you find a woman both
More lovely and more virtuous than I,
You may, upon this one condition,
Marry her with my permission.'
She thought, so certain of her charms was she,

That such an oath would be a guarantee
(Though got by cunning) that he would refrain
From ever marrying again.
The King burst into tears and vowed
To do whatever she desired.

She in his arms forthwith expired,
And never did a husband weep so loud.
By night and day his sobs came thick and fast.
The courtiers judged his sorrow could not last;
He wept, they said, as if he wished to see
The mourning done as promptly as might be.
The court proved right. Some months went past,
And then the King announced he thought it good
To choose another consort if he could.
He had a tricky problem now
Because he had to keep his vow;
And therefore any wife he found
Must be at least as fair of face,
As well endowed with wit and grace,
As was the first, now underground.

But not at court, though beauties there abound,
Nor in the towns or countryside,
Nor in neighbouring lands beside,
Was any other woman seen
As lovely as the former queen,
Except her daughter; she alone
With young and tender beauties of her own,
Possessed attractions that the Queen had lacked.
The King, now mad with love, observed the fact,
And got the crazy notion in his head
That he and the Princess should therefore wed.
An expert casuist* he found contended
That such a match, perhaps, could be defended.

*The courtiers attempt to rouse their king* ☞

But she was much disturbed, and had no rest
On hearing sentiments like these expressed;
She sobbed and wept by day and night.
She went, with sad and weary heart,
To tell her godmother about her plight.
This fairy's dwelling, set apart,
Was in a distant grotto, filled
With coral, pearls, and shells; in magic art
Her godmother was very skilled.

(What fairies were in olden times
You will not need to learn from me;
Your Grandma told you on her knee,
Along with tales and nursery rhymes.)

She said, on seeing her: 'My dear,
I know why you're so sad, and why you're here,
But now you're with me, have no fear.
Nothing will do you harm, provided
That you will let yourself be guided
By my advice. Your father, it is true,
Has said he wants to marry you.
To ask for such a thing is mad;
If you agree, that's just as bad.
To thwart him, while not seeming to refuse,
We'll circumvent his folly with a ruse.
You need to say you won't consent
To marry till you're quite content
With what you ask him now to give: a dress
The colour of the heavens*—something which,
However great he is, however rich,
Though Heaven has always given him success,
Will prove beyond his powers to do.'

*An expert casuist defends the match*

The Princess, trembling through and through,
To give this message went her way.
The King, without the least delay,
Called dressmakers across the land,
And made them clearly understand
That what he wanted was a dress,
Sky-coloured, for the young Princess;
And further that they'd best not make him wait
More than a day before the job was done,
For if they did, as sure as fate,
He'd send them to the gallows, every one.
Before the sun rose on the second morn
The precious dress was ready to be worn:
Its sheer and splendid azure hue
Outshone the sky's most glorious blue
When clouds are strewn across it golden bright.

The Princess, with more sorrow than delight,
Is lost for words; she's very much afraid
She'll have to keep the bargain that she's made.
'You've got to ask him for another boon,'
She hears her fairy godmother declare:
'No common gift this time, but rare:
A dress the colour of the moon;
He cannot give it.' But her new demand
At once becomes the monarch's next command.
He calls embroiderers: 'Diana's globe
Will shine at night more dimly than this robe;
Within four days, the work must be complete,'
He says; and in four days, it's at his feet,
And just as beautiful as he'd required.
The moon when skies are clear, attired
In silver for her evening parade,
So bright she makes the stars and planets fade,
Is less superb and radiant than the dress.

Astonished and admiring, the Princess
Was almost ready to give in; but then,
Encouraged by her godmother again,
She asked another gift—a better one;
'My lord,' she said, 'with this I'll be content:
I want a dress the colour of the sun.'
In his excess of love, her father sent
To fetch the finest jeweller that there was.
'Make me this gleaming dress,' the man was told,
'In cloth all sewn with diamonds and gold;
And do it well,' the King went on, 'because,
If not, you'll die of torture, have no doubt.'
The threat was never carried out:
The man was disinclined to shirk.
He sent the precious piece of work
Within a week. So splendid was this dress
That bright-haired Phoebus, when across the skies
He drives his chariot of gold, is less
Ablaze with light, and dazzles less our eyes.

Dumbfounded by these gifts, the poor Princess
Finds no reply to thwart her king and lord.
Her godmother is close at hand: 'My dear,
You can't stop now,' she whispers in her ear;
'There's nothing that your father can't afford;
You know he has the donkey still,
Which while it's there will always fill
His treasury with crowns of gold.
Just ask him for the creature's skin.
Since that is what his wealth is in,
This gift, I'm sure, is one that he'll withhold.'

The fairy was extremely wise,
No doubt, but failed to realize

That lovers never count the cost
Of all the gold and silver lost
If once their passion gains its prize.
The monarch, therefore, gallantly complied
And met his daughter's wish; the donkey died.

They bring the skin to her: she's filled with dread,
And bitterly bewails the fate that lies ahead;
But then her godmother appears:
'Those who do good,' she says, 'need have no fears.
First you must lead your father to believe
That you will share with him the married state;
But on the wedding day, alone, you'll leave:
You must not risk so horrible a fate;
Go in disguise to some far distant place.
Here now,' she added, 'is your travelling case.
It's large enough to hold your dressing things,
Your brushes, mirror, rubies, diamond rings,
And all your clothes; moreover here's my wand
For you to use. The casket will respond
By following wherever you may go,
But secretly, deep in the ground below.
Then should you want to see the chest,
Just take the wand and keep it pressed
Against the earth, and then and there
The chest will magically appear.
To guard yourself from prying eyes,
The donkey-skin's a fine disguise,
For nobody could ever guess,
Seeing you in so foul a dress,
That such a filthy thing could hide
Someone so beautiful inside.'

Thus camouflaged, the Princess went away,
Bidding the fairy many fond farewells,
In the cool air of morning. On that day
The King had hoped to hear the wedding bells
Ring out in joy; but he's bereft;
They tell him that his bride has left.

Each house, each street, each avenue
Was rigorously searched, and searched again;
But all the agitation was in vain,
For how or where she'd vanished, no one knew.
A sad, despondent mood spread all about:
No wedding meant no cakes, no sweets, no feast;
The ladies of the court were much put out,
And hardly ate a thing; as for the priest,
His meal was late and meagre; what was worse,
No church collection helped to fill his purse.

Journeying onwards all this time
Her face besmeared with dirt and grime,
The Princess begged from passers-by.
On coming to a house, she'd try
To get herself a servant's place,
But when they saw her grubby face,
Together with the skin she wore,
The wives she asked, however poor,
However coarse, would shut the door.
So on she trudged, and on and on, until
She reached a farmhouse where the wife required
A serving-girl with just sufficient skill
To do the lowest chores; and she was hired,
To wash the rags and keep the pig-trough clean.
A corner of the kitchen, dark and mean,
Became her home, and here she had to mix

With farmhands, oafs, and louts, who played her tricks
At every turn; they harassed her,
Tormented her, embarrassed her;
She was the butt of all their rustic fun,
Of every joke and every stupid pun.
She had on Sundays some few hours of rest.
She had a little work to do, no more;
Returning to her room, she barred the door.
She'd wash away the grime, and from the chest
Would take her toilet-cloth, and lots
Of creams and lotions neatly stored in pots.
The looking-glass she'd carefully arrange,
Then stood before it, happy, full of pride,
Wearing each dress in turn. The first she tried
Was like the moon, all silver. Then she'd change,
And wear the dress that brilliantly outshone
The sun itself; then finally put on
The azure dress whose gorgeous hue
Surpassed the heavens' purest blue.
The trouble was, the room could not contain
Each dress's generously flowing train.
It was a joy to gaze at her reflection
And see herself so beautifully dressed:
She thought that with her pure complexion
She must look finer than the rest,
Which kept her spirits up till next weekend.

Something I may have failed to mention
Is that the farmyard had a large extension
In which innumerable birds were penned:
An aviary; the King, who liked display,
Showed off his riches in this way,
With musk-fed geese* and cormorants and quails,
And little bustards, bantam hens, and rails,

*The Princess laments her sad situation*

Birds of a thousand kinds or more,
Each stranger than the one before,
Filling a dozen courtyards in their cages.
The monarch's son would come with friends and pages
To rest awhile in this delightful place
And take cool drinks, when thirsty from the chase.
This Prince's martial looks did not resemble
Those of the fair Adonis: regal his mien,
And fierce his glance; the bravest foes would tremble
Before him in the field. Thus was he seen
By Donkey-Skin, with tender admiration;
Watching afar, she knew that for her part,
Despite the dirt and squalor of her station,
Her feelings proved she had a royal heart.
'He truly has a prince's air,'
She thought, 'while seeming not to care
About his greatness. And how much
He merits love! Oh happy she
Whose beauty and whose love might touch
His heart and keep it hers! And as for me,
I'd sooner wear the meanest, poorest dress
That he might give, than any I possess.'

This Prince, when walking, came one day,
Among the courtyards where the birds were kept,
Upon a door along a passageway,
And this was where the Princess slept.
The keyhole as it chanced was at a height
Just right to look through. As it chanced,
The day was Sunday too; so when he glanced
Into her room, he saw a wondrous sight:
The diamonds lay round her neck; and spun
From gold, her dress was dazzling like the sun.
The Prince stood there transfixed in contemplation;

Scarce could he breathe, so great his admiration.
And yet, despite the gorgeous clothes she wore,
Her countenance attracted him much more:
Its perfect outline, full of grace,
Her young complexion, fresh and clear,
Gave sweet expression to her face;
Besides, so virtuous did she appear,
With dignity and modesty combined,
The outward signs of beauty in the mind,
That her demeanour played the greatest part
In making her the mistress of his heart.

Three times from sudden love he raised his fist
Against the door, but only to desist:
Three times respect made him withdraw;
It seemed a goddess that he saw.
Back to the palace he made his pensive way,
To sigh and languish there by night and day.
The Carnival has started: he rejects
All invitations to the dance; objects
To theatre; hunting he abominates;
The most alluring food he hates.
And as he mournfully repines,
He's lost in apathy, his health declines.
One day he asked the unknown beauty's name.
'Who can she be, this lovely nymph, whose room
Is in that nasty alley deep in gloom
Beyond the poultry-yard?' The answer came:
'It must be Donkey-Skin you mean,'
They said; 'but she's no nymph; and "Donkey-Skin"
She's called because it's what she dresses in.
An uglier brute you've never seen.
A she-wolf's prettier than her, for sure;
If love's an illness, she's the perfect cure.'

Much else they say, but all in vain.
Her image now is deeply traced
Inside his mind, and cannot be effaced:
He's caught by love; he'll not be free again.

Meanwhile the Queen his mother cannot rest,
Seeing her son so gloomy and depressed.
The Prince, though plunged in grief, will not disclose
The reason for these most distressing woes,
And when she tenderly enquires
Says only this: what he desires
Is just that Donkey-Skin should bake,
For him and him alone, a cake.
His mother cannot take it in,
And asks: 'Who is this Donkey-Skin?'
'Oh Heavens!—her?' they said, 'oh dear!
Dear Madam, she's a miserable slut!
A dirtier beast you'll not find anywhere:
A proper slattern!'—'That's as may be; but,'
The Queen said, 'if my son desires a dish
Prepared by her, I'll see he gets his wish.'
(If he had asked, she loved him so, you see,
He would have had gold coins for tea.)

So Donkey-Skin became a cook.
Butter and salt and eggs she took,
Inside the hovel where she lived,
With flour most scrupulously sieved
(She knew that when it's sifted fine
The mixture's easy to combine),
And having washed herself she shed
From off her shoulders, arms, and head
Her dirty, shaggy camouflage,
And took instead a fine corsage

Of silver which she neatly laced
To wear around her slender waist,
And thus attired, began to cook.
By chance—some say she didn't look—
A ring she had of flawless gold,
And happened to be wearing, fell
Into the cake; though I've been told,
By those who know the story well,
That Donkey-Skin intended it to fall.
To me that's not impossible at all,
For speaking honestly I'm sure
That when the Prince, outside her door,
Had stood that time while peeping through,
She knew it; women always do.
A woman's senses are so keen,
She's so alert, that if your eye should chance
To rest on her a moment, then your glance
Will be observed; she'll sense that she's been seen.
And then there is another thing:
The Princess, when she dropped her ring—
Unless I'm very much deceived;
In fact I'd swear to it—believed
That what she'd hidden for her lover
He'd be most happy to discover.

And never did a woman make
A softer, more enticing cake.
He tasted it with much delight,
Then gobbled it; and truth to tell,
He nearly ate the ring as well,
So wolfish was his appetite.
But when he found it and beheld
Its gorgeous emerald stone, his bosom swelled
With greater joy: the little golden band

Seemed still to hold the beauty of her hand.
He put it by his pillow where he slept,
In order that his secret should be kept.
Yet visibly meanwhile his health declined,
And doctors of experience and skill,
As he grew thinner, with one voice opined
That it was love that made the Prince so ill.

Now touching marriage, hostile things are said;
But nonetheless, for maladies like this
The recommended cure is married bliss;
It was resolved, therefore, that he should wed.
He seemed a while reluctant, then replied:
'Upon this one condition, I'll agree:
That she whose finger fits this ring must be
The woman that you give me for my bride.'
The King's and Queen's surprise was very great,
But seeing that the Prince's state
Was sad indeed, they judged it best
Not to refuse his strange request.
At once a search is ordered by the King
To find the finger that will fit the ring,
And much improve its owner's situation,
However low or high her social station.

Each maiden's purpose now becomes the same;
All have to bring their fingers to be tried;
None thinks another has a better claim.
In order, though (so rumour says), to win
The Prince's heart and be his bride,
The finger needs to be extremely thin,
And charlatans sell recipes to render
The fingers of the buyers very slender.
One lady, by a monstrous whim,

Decides to make her fingers slim
By scraping them, as she might trim
Some carrots; while another snips
Small pieces from her finger-tips.
Then with a press another tries
By squeezing to reduce their size.
Another yet, to make them thin,
Obtains some acid, dips them in,
And lets it burn away the skin.
These ladies will try anything
To make a finger fit the ring.

The tests commence: first come the young princesses,
The duchesses, and then the marchionesses.
Fine hands they have, but just a little thick:
Not fine enough, it seems, to do the trick.
Daughters of barons next, of counts and earls,
Of lesser gentry too; to no avail:
Like others higher in the social scale,
Their fingers are too big. Then come the girls
Of lower birth and duller dress,
But not of less attractiveness.
Their fingers, though, at each attempt,
When shape and fit appear, this time, just right,
All fail; the ring appears to show contempt,
And slips or sticks: too loose, or else too tight.
So then they had to let the rest apply:
The servants and the maids, the lesser fry,
Whose hands are red and roughened by the tub,
Who have the clothes to wash, the floors to scrub,
The poultry-yard to clean—in fact the lot.
The prize is just as much for them to win,
They think, as for some miss with smoother skin.
Many a girl with fingers broad and squat

Made her appearance then to try
The prince's ring, with no more hope
Than if she thought to take a rope
And thread it through a needle's eye.
It seemed that nothing more could then be done,
For all had tried the ring, except for one:
Still working in the kitchen, quite neglected,
Was Donkey-Skin. 'And she can't be expected,'
They said, 'to wed the Prince and reign
As queen, that's absolutely plain.'
'Why not?' replied the Prince; 'let her appear.'
Then laughter spread among the crowd,
And everyone exclaimed aloud:
'What can he mean? Allow her here,
That filthy creature? What a joke!'
But when from underneath the cloak
Of rough and dirty skin she drew
A hand like ivory, shot through
With just a touch of rosy pink,
Then nobody knew what to think;
And next, before their unbelieving eyes,
Her finger slid into the fateful ring,
And fitted it; which caused no small surprise.
They thought they'd better take her to the King,
But first, she said, in order to appear
Before her royal master and her lord,
There was a single favour she implored:
To find herself some other clothes to wear.
And now the courtiers thought to mock,
And laugh their fill at Donkey-Skin's new frock;
But when, once in the palace, she proceeded
From room to room, and wore a splendid gown,
Superbly beautiful, which far exceeded
All dresses ever known in court or town,

With on her head the diamonds shining bright
Which made each golden hair a ray of light,
With azure eyes, whose sweet and noble fire,
Bewitching, proud, were certain to inspire
Love with every glance; and when her waist,
So slender that it might have been embraced
Between a man's two hands: when all, at last,
Was seen divinely fair, she far surpassed
The courtly ladies in their fine array;
Their beauties simply seemed to fade away.

Loudly the crowd rejoiced on every side;
The worthy King could scarce contain his glee
Seeing the beauty of the wife-to-be:
The Queen already doted on the bride.
As for the love-lorn Prince, their son and heir,
The passage in so short a time
From misery to joy sublime
Was almost more than he could bear.

Then all looked forward to the wedding day
And started to prepare without delay;
The kings and queens around had invitations:
Bedecked in ornaments of every kind,
Leaving their native lands behind
They rode to join the celebrations.
From far and wide they came; among them, some
Had journeyed from Aurora's distant lands*
Mounted on elephants; others had come
Out of Arabia's desert coasts and sands:
So dark and ugly that they made
The children very much afraid;
And all these guests, their numbers growing,
Soon filled the court to overflowing.

*Kings and queens from distant lands arrive for the wedding celebrations* ☞

But none, of any prince or potentate,
Arrived in more resplendent state
Than did the father of the bride.
Though once in love, he'd cast aside
The passion burning up his soul like fire;
He'd banished any criminal desire,
And of those hateful wishes, now suppressed,
All that remained served only to inspire
Deeper devotion in his breast.
On seeing her he weeps: 'Now Heaven be blessed,
My dearest child,' he cries, 'that by its grace
We meet again, and that I am allowed
To see you here!' They joyously embrace:
Their joy is shared by all the crowd.
The groom is just as pleased and proud
That marriage to his love will bring
Alliance with a mighty king.
Just then the fairy godmother arrives,
To tell them all, in full, the story
Of Donkey-Skin, and thus contrives
To cover her with greater glory.

There are some lessons that a child may learn
From listening to this tale: they won't take long;
And first that sufferings, however stern,
Are preferable by far to doing wrong;
And next, whatever trials life may send
Virtue will always triumph in the end;
Also that love deranged defies all sense:
Against it, reason is a poor defence;
Lovers, extravagant beyond all measure,
Will give away for love their dearest treasure.

Again: young ladies may be fed
On nothing but the coarsest bread
Provided that, besides such fare,
They have some pretty clothes to wear;
And not a woman anywhere
Will not believe that she's as fair
As all the rest; and in addition
Has never dreamt that when of old
They held that famous competition
To win the apple made of gold,*
If she'd been there, as goddesses paraded,
She surely would have looked as good as they did,
Or better still, and would have been
Paris's choice as beauty queen.

This tale is hard to credit, to be sure,
But yet, as long as children dwell
Upon this earth, with mums and grans as well,
Its memory will stay secure.

# STORIES OR TALES
OF
## BYGONE TIMES
WITH THEIR MORALS

Mademoiselle:

It will not seem strange that a child should have entertained himself by composing the tales in this collection, but it will be astonishing that he should have had the audacity to present them to you.

However, Mademoiselle, notwithstanding the huge discrepancy between the simplicity of the stories and the brilliance of your mind, it will appear, if the tales are properly examined, that I am not as blameworthy as I might seem. The moral lessons that they all contain are extremely sensible, and will be understood more or less easily according as my readers are more or less perceptive; and furthermore, seeing that there is no greater sign of mental capacity than the ability both to rise to the greatest heights and descend to everyday matters, nobody will be surprised that a great Princess, who by nature and education has become familiar with the most elevated ideas, should condescend to divert herself with bagatelles such as these.

I know that the tales give a portrayal of life in the humblest families, where the laudable desire to provide early instruction to the young has led to the creation of stories which, bereft of reason, are therefore suitable for children, since in them reason is still lacking; but for whom could it be more suitable to study the people's way of life than for those destined to lead them? Heroes, including heroes from among your own ancestors,* have been impelled, by their desire to know about such things, to enter cabins and hovels in order to see with their own eyes the detail of the lives that were led in them, such knowledge having seemed to them necessary if their education was to be complete.

However that may be, Mademoiselle—

*Though fairy stories cannot be believed,*
*To whom could I more fittingly appeal*
*To prove that what they tell us might be real?*
*For nobody could ever have conceived,*
*Since fairies gave their gifts so long ago,*
*That any of them might bestow*
*So many gifts, such talents too,*
*As Nature has bestowed on you.*

I remain, Mademoiselle, with the most profound respect, the very faithful humble servant of Your Royal Highness,

P. DARMANCOUR.*

# The Sleeping Beauty
# in the Wood

❧❧❧

O NCE upon a time there lived a king and queen who were
ever so unhappy, because they had no children; so unhappy
I can't tell you. They went to all the spas to drink the waters
there, gave presents to all the saints, went on pilgrimages, and
always said their prayers; everything was tried and nothing
worked. But at last the Queen did become pregnant, and had a
baby daughter. They held a beautiful service for her to be chris-
tened; all the fairies they could find in the country were to come
(there were seven of them), to be godmothers for the little
Princess, which meant that each would bestow a gift on her,
which was the custom for fairies in those days, and then she
would be as perfect as you could possibly imagine.

When the christening service was finished, all the guests went
back to the royal palace, where a banquet was to be given in
honour of the fairies. Each of them had her place laid magnificently at table with a solid gold case, which contained a knife, a
fork, and a spoon made out of pure gold, and decorated with
diamonds and rubies. But as everyone was sitting down to table,
they saw an aged fairy come in, who had not been invited, because
for more than fifty years she had never left the tower she lived
in, so that she was believed to be dead, or under a spell. The
King had a place laid for her at table, but there was no means of
giving her a case of solid gold like the others, because only
seven cases had been made, one for each of the seven. The aged
fairy believed herself insulted, and muttered threatening words
between her teeth. Sitting beside her, one of the younger fairies
heard what she said, and guessed that the gift that she would give

to the little Princess might be dangerous for her; so she went and hid behind a tapestry on the wall as soon as the meal was finished, in order to speak last of all, and prevent if possible any harm that the old fairy might do.

Meanwhile the fairies began to present their gifts to the Princess. The gift that the youngest fairy gave was that she would be the loveliest person in the world; the next one's gift was that she would be as clever as an angel; the third gift was that she would do everything with all the grace imaginable; the fourth that she would dance to perfection; the fifth that she would sing like a nightingale; and the sixth, that she would play beautiful music on all kinds of instruments. When it came to the turn of the very old fairy, whose head was shaking, but not so much from age as from bad temper, she said that the Princess would prick her hand on the point of the spindle on a spinning-wheel, and that she would die.

This terrible gift made the whole company shudder, and they all began to weep. It was then that the younger fairy stepped out from behind the tapestry, and in a loud voice she spoke these words: 'Oh King and Queen, be reassured; your daughter will not die, although it is not in my power to undo completely what the older fairy has done. The Princess will prick her hand on a spindle, but instead of dying, she will fall into a deep sleep. It will last for a hundred years, and at the end of that time the son of a king will come to waken her.' In order to try to prevent the disaster announced by the old fairy, the King at once had an edict proclaimed, by which every person was forbidden to spin wool on a spinning-wheel or keep a spindle at home, on pain of death.

Fifteen or sixteen years went by, and one day, when the King and Queen were on a visit to one of their summer residences, it happened that the Princess, in running about the castle and going from apartment to apartment, went higher and higher up a tower. She came to a tiny attic room and found an old woman sitting

*The Princess finds an old woman spinning alone*

alone, spinning wool from her distaff. This good lady had never heard that the King had forbidden everyone to use a spindle.

'What is it that you are doing there, good woman?' asked the Princess.

'I am spinning, my pretty child,' said the old woman, not knowing who she was talking to.

'What fun!' the Princess said then, 'how do you do it? Give it to me and let me see if I can do it too.'

She took the spindle; and because she was hasty and impulsive, and in any case the fairies' decree had decided what would happen, no sooner had she done so than she pricked her hand and fell down in a faint. The good woman was very upset and cried out for help; people came from everywhere, and splashed water on the Princess's face, loosened her clothes, slapped her wrists, and rubbed her temples with eau-de-cologne; but nothing could revive her. The King had come at once on hearing all the noise, and remembered the fairies' prediction. He realized that it had to happen, because the fairies had said it would, and ordered that the Princess should be placed in the finest apartment in the castle, on a bed embroidered with gold and silver. You would have said she was an angel, she looked so beautiful. Fainting had not taken away the fresh colours from her face; her cheeks were rosy pink and her lips like coral. It was only that her eyes were closed; but you could tell that she was not dead because she could still be heard breathing gently. The King gave orders that she was to be left to sleep in peace until the time for her to be awakened should arrive.

The good fairy who, in order to save her life, had condemned her to sleep for a hundred years, was twelve thousand leagues away in the Kingdom of Matakin when the Princess had her accident, but she was given the news in an instant by a little dwarf with seven-league boots (these were boots in which you could go seven leagues in a single stride). The fairy set off at once and appeared at the castle an hour later in a chariot of fire drawn by dragons. The King went to help her down from the chariot, and she gave her approval to everything he had done; but, possessing great foresight, she reflected that when the Princess awoke from her sleep she would find things very difficult all alone in the old castle; and this is what she did. With her wand, she touched everyone in the castle except the King and Queen: governesses, maids of honour, ladies' maids, gentlemen of the household, stewards, footmen, cooks, scullions, turnspits, guards, pages, doormen; she also touched all the horses in the stables, the ostlers there, the great guard-dogs in the stable-yard, and little Puff, the Princess's lapdog, who was lying beside her on her bed. As soon as she touched them they all fell asleep, not to wake up until their mistress did, so as to be ready to serve her when they were needed. Even the spits in front of the kitchen fire, all covered with pheasants and partridges, went to sleep, and the fire did too.

This all happened in a moment; fairies did not take long over their work. Then the King and Queen, after having kissed their daughter without awakening her, left the castle. They issued orders that nobody should come near. But the ban was not needed, because within a quarter of an hour so many trees had shot up, large and small, all around the castle park, with brambles and thorns all intertwined, that neither man nor beast could have got through. All that could still be seen was the top of the castle towers, and only from a long way off. No doubt this was another of the fairy's devices to make sure that the Princess would have nothing to fear from inquisitive visitors while she was asleep.

A hundred years later, the son of the king then ruling, who was not of the same family as the sleeping Princess, went hunting in that region. Seeing some towers rising above a tall dense wood, he asked what they were. Everyone present answered according to what he had heard tell. Some said that it was an ancient castle where ghosts were seen to walk; others, that all the witches round about held their sabbaths there. The commonest opinion was that it was where an ogre lived, and where he brought all the children he could catch, in order to eat them in peace without being followed, since he alone had the power to make his way through the wood. The Prince did not know what to believe; but then an elderly peasant began to speak, saying: 'Your Highness: more than fifty years ago, I heard my father say that in the castle there lay a Princess, who was the most beautiful in the world; she was to stay asleep for a hundred years, and would be awakened by the son of a king, for whom she was destined.' The young Prince took fire at the old man's words: he took it for granted at once that it was he who would succeed in this splendid adventure, and inspired by love and glory he resolved to find out at once how things stood.

He had scarcely taken his first step towards the wood than all the great trees, brambles and thorns drew aside of themselves to let him pass. He set out towards the castle, which he could see at the end of a long avenue ahead, and was a little surprised to see that none of his servants had been able to follow him; the trees had closed behind him as soon as he passed. He continued on his way regardless, for a young and ardent prince is always full of courage. He came into a great forecourt, where everything that met his eyes was such as to freeze his blood with fear. The silence was terrible, and the look of death was all around. Nothing was to be seen but the bodies of men and animals lying stretched out, who appeared to be dead. He could tell nonetheless, from the blotchy noses and flushed complexions of the Swiss guards,* that they were only sleeping, and the dregs of wine left in their glasses showed clearly enough that they had fallen asleep in the middle of having a drink.

Through a great court paved with marble he went, up a flight of steps, and entered the guardroom, where the guards were standing in line, their guns on their shoulders, and snoring with all their might. He passed through several rooms full of gentlemen and ladies, all asleep, some standing and some sitting; he came to a room that was all of gold, and saw on a bed, with its curtains drawn back to leave it open, the most beautiful sight that he had ever seen: a Princess who seemed to be about fifteen or sixteen years old, and who in her radiant splendour had something luminous and divine about her. Trembling with wonder and admiration, he approached and knelt down beside her.

Since the end of the enchantment had come, the Princess woke up, and gazing at him with greater tenderness in her eyes than might have seemed proper at a first meeting, she said: 'Is that you, my prince? What a long time you have kept me waiting!' Delighted at these words, and still more by the tone in which she said them, the Prince did not know how to express his gratitude and joy, but he told her that he loved her more than himself. Although what he said was badly expressed it pleased her all the more; the greatest love is the least eloquent. Of the two of them, she was the less tongue-tied, which is not surprising since she had had the time to think of what she would say; for it is likely (though history is silent on the matter) that during her long sleep the good fairy had seen to it that she enjoyed sweet dreams. Be that as it may,* they spent four hours talking to each other and still had not said the half of what they wanted.

In the meantime, the whole palace had awakened with the Princess. Everyone's thoughts were on getting back to work, and since they were not in love, they were all dying of hunger. The lady-in-waiting, famished like the rest of them, grew impatient, and said loudly to the Princess that her meal was served. The Prince helped the Princess to her feet; she was fully dressed and her clothes were magnificent, but he took good care not to tell her that she was dressed like Grandmother in the old days, with a starched high collar; it did not make her any the less beautiful. They went into a hall lined with mirrors, where they had their supper, and were served by the officers of the Princess's household. The violins and oboes played old pieces of music, which

*The Prince passes gentlemen and ladies, all asleep* ☞

were excellent, even though they had not been played for almost a hundred years. After supper, without wasting time, the High Chaplain married them in the castle chapel, and the lady-in-waiting drew the bed-curtain. They slept little, for the Princess had little need of it, and the Prince left her as soon as it was morning to return to the town, since his father would be anxious about him.

The Prince told him that he had got lost in the forest while out hunting, and that he had spent the night in a hovel belonging to a charcoal-burner, who had given him cheese and black bread to eat. The King, who was a good soul, believed him, but his mother was not convinced. She noticed that he went hunting almost every day, and always had some excuse to give when he had slept away from home for two or three nights; so she became certain that he was carrying on some love-affair, for he lived in this way with the Princess for more than two whole years, and had two children with her. The first was a girl, and was named Dawn; and the second, who was a boy, was called Day, since he looked even more beautiful than his sister.

The Queen said to her son several times, in the hope of drawing him out, that one should enjoy oneself in life, but he never dared to entrust her with his secret; although he loved her, he was afraid of her, because she came from a family of ogres, and the King had married her only because of her great wealth. It was even whispered at court that she herself had ogreish tendencies, and that when she saw small children going by she found it almost impossible to prevent herself from jumping on them, which is why the Prince would never say anything. But when the King died, which happened after another two years, and the Prince was in command, he made his marriage public, and went in a grand procession to fetch the Queen his wife from her castle. A magnificent reception was held for her in the capital, where she made her entrance into the town accompanied by her two children.

*The Prince sees the beautiful Princess*

Some time later, the new King went to war against his neighbour the Emperor Cantalabutto. He left the government of the kingdom in the hands of the Queen his mother, asking her to take special care of his wife and children, for he was to be away at the war for the whole summer. As soon as he had left, the Queen Mother sent her daughter-in-law and the children to a summer residence she had in the forest, so as to satisfy her horrible desires more easily. She went there herself a few days later, and said one evening to her steward: 'Tomorrow evening for supper, I want to eat little Dawn.'

'Alas, my lady!' said the steward.

'That is my wish,' said the Queen, and her tone was the tone of an ogress who wants fresh meat, 'and I want to eat her with onion and mustard sauce.' The poor man, realizing that an ogress was not to be trifled with, took a great knife and went up to little Dawn's room. She was then four years old, and came across the room skipping and laughing to embrace him and ask him for sweets. Tears came to his eyes, the knife fell from his hands, and he went down to the farmyard and cut the throat of a small lamb, which he served up to his mistress with such a good sauce that she assured him that she had never tasted anything as good. He had taken away little Dawn at the same time, and gave her to his wife to hide in their lodgings at the end of the farmyard.

A week later, the wicked Queen said to the steward: 'I want to eat little Day for my supper.' He did not protest, but resolved to trick her again as he had before. He went to look for little Day, and found him with a small sword in his hand, practising fencing against a fat monkey, although he was only three years old. The steward took him to his wife, who hid him with little Dawn, and instead of the little boy he served up a tender young kid, which the ogress found excellent.

Everything had gone well until then, but one evening the wicked Queen said to the steward: 'I want to eat the young Queen, cooked in the same sauce as her children.' This time the poor steward despaired of being able to deceive her: the young Queen was more than twenty years old, not counting the hundred years when she had been asleep, and her skin was somewhat tough, although it was fine and white. How was he to find, among the animals kept for eating,* one as tough as that? He took the decision, in order to save his own life, to cut the Queen's throat, and went up to her room with the intention of getting it over and done with. He worked himself up into a rage and entered the Queen's room with his dagger in his hand. However, he did not want to kill her without any warning, and told her, with great respect, of the orders he had received from the Queen Mother.

'Do your duty,' she said, stretching out her neck; 'carry out the command you have been given. Then I shall see my children again, my poor children, whom I loved so much.' She believed them dead, because, when they were taken away, nobody had told her anything.

'No, my lady, no,' said the poor steward in tears, 'you will not die, and I will make sure that you do see your beloved children, though it will be in my house, where I have hidden them, and I will deceive the Queen again by giving her a young doe to eat instead.' At once he took her to his house, where he left her to embrace her children and weep with them, and went to prepare the doe for cooking; the Queen ate it for supper with as much relish as if it had been the young Queen. She was very pleased with her cruel deeds, and meant to tell the King, on his return, that ravening wolves had eaten his wife and the two children.

One evening, when she was prowling about the castle's courtyards and farmyards as usual, in order to catch the scent of any fresh meat, she heard little Day who was crying in a basement room, because the Queen his mother had said that she would have him whipped for being naughty; she could also hear little Dawn, who was pleading for her brother to be forgiven.

The ogress, recognizing the voices of the young Queen and her children, was furious to have been tricked.

The next morning she ordered, in a dreadful voice that made everyone shudder, that a huge cauldron was to be brought into the middle of the main courtyard and filled with toads* and vipers and snakes of every sort, for the young Queen and her children to be thrown into it, together with the steward, his wife, and their maidservant; she had given the order to have them led out with their hands tied behind their backs.

They were standing there, with the executioners getting ready to throw them into the cauldron, when the King, who was not expected so soon, rode into the courtyard; he had changed horses at every stage for speed. In amazement, he asked what this horrible spectacle could mean. Nobody dared to explain. And it was then that the ogress, maddened by what she saw before her, flung herself head first into the cauldron, and was devoured in an instant by the horrid creatures she had put there. Despite everything, the King was upset: she was his mother; but he soon consoled himself with his beautiful wife and children.

### THE MORAL OF THIS TALE

> For girls to wait awhile, so they may wed
> A loving husband, handsome, rich, and kind:
> That's natural enough, I'd say;
> But just the same, to stay in bed
> A hundred years asleep—you'll never find
> Such patience in a girl today.

> Another lesson may be meant:
> Lovers lose nothing if they wait,
> And tie the knot of marriage late;
> They'll not be any less content.

Young girls, though, yearn for married bliss
So ardently, that for my part
I cannot find it in my heart
To preach a doctrine such as this.

# Little Red Riding-Hood

❦❦❦

O NCE upon a time, in a village, there lived a little girl, the
prettiest you could wish to see. Her mother adored her,
and her grandmother adored her even more. This kind lady had
a riding-hood* made for her granddaughter; it was red, and it
suited her so well that everywhere she went she was called Little
Red Riding-Hood.

One day, when her mother had done some baking, she made
some buns,* and said: 'Go and see how your grandmama is,
because I've heard she isn't well. Take her one of these buns,
and a little pot of butter.' Little Red Riding-Hood set off at once
to visit her grandmother, who lived in another village. As she
was going into a wood, she met Master Wolf, and he wanted
very much to eat her up; but he did not dare, because there were
some woodcutters in the forest. He asked her where she was
going. The poor child, who did not know that it is dangerous to
stay and listen to a wolf, told him: 'I am going to see my grandmother, and I'm taking her a bun and a little pot of butter that
my mother is sending me with.'

'Does she live a long way off?' asked the Wolf.

'Oh yes,' said Little Red Riding-Hood, 'it's beyond the mill
that you can see ever so far away over there, and it's the first
house you come to in the village.'

'Well then,' said the Wolf, 'I'd like to go and see her too. I'll
go by this path here, and you go by that one, and we'll see who
gets there first.'

The Wolf began to run as hard as he could along his path,
which was shorter, while the little girl went by the longer path,
and amused herself gathering hazel-nuts, running after butter-
flies, and making posies out of the flowers that she saw.

*Little Red Riding-Hood meets Master Wolf*

The Wolf did not take long to reach the grandmother's house. He knocked at the door, rat-a-tat-tat!

'Who is it?'

'It's me, your granddaughter, Little Red Riding-Hood,' said the Wolf, imitating the little girl's voice, 'and I've brought you a bun and a little pot of butter that Mummy has sent.'

The kind grandmother, who was in bed because she was not feeling very well, called out: 'Draw the peg back, and the bar will fall.'* The Wolf drew the peg back and the door opened. He flung himself on the old lady, and ate her all up in less than a moment, because he had not had a meal for more than three days. Then he shut the door, went to lie down in the grandmother's bed, and waited for Little Red Riding-Hood. In a little while she came, and knocked on the door, rat-a-tat-tat!

'Who is it?'

Little Red Riding-Hood, hearing the Wolf's gruff voice, was frightened at first, but, believing that her grandmother had a cold, she answered: 'It's me, your granddaughter, Little Red Riding-Hood, and I've brought you a bun and a little pot of butter that Mummy has sent.'

Making his voice a little softer, the Wolf called out: 'Draw the peg back, and the bar will fall.' Little Red Riding-Hood drew the peg back and the door opened. When he saw her coming in, the Wolf hid under the bedclothes, and said: 'Put the bun and the little pot of butter on the chest, and come and get into bed with me.'

Little Red Riding-Hood undressed and got into the bed, where she was very surprised to see what her grandmother looked like without any clothes on, and she said:

'Oh grandmama, what long arms you have!'

'All the better to hug you with, my dear.'

'Oh grandmama, what long legs you have!'

'All the better for running with, my dear.'

'Oh grandmama, what big ears you have!'

*The Wolf flings himself on the old lady, and eats her all up*

'All the better to hear you with, my dear.'
'Oh grandmama, what big eyes you have!'
'All the better to see you with, my dear.'
'Oh grandmama, what great big teeth you have!'
'And they are all the better to EAT YOU WITH!'*

And as he said these words, the wicked Wolf flung himself on Little Red Riding-Hood, and ate her up.

## THE MORAL OF THIS TALE

Young children, as this tale will show,
And mainly pretty girls with charm,
Do wrong and often come to harm
In letting those they do not know
Stay talking to them when they meet.
And if they don't do as they ought,
It's no surprise that some are caught
By wolves who take them off to eat.

I call them wolves, but you will find
That some are not the savage kind,
Not howling, ravening or raging;
Their manners seem, instead, engaging,
They're softly-spoken and discreet.
Young ladies whom they talk to on the street
They follow to their homes and through the hall,
And upstairs to their rooms;* when they're there
They're not as friendly as they might appear:
These are the most dangerous wolves of all.

*Little Red Riding-Hood is surprised to see what her grandmother looks like*

# Bluebeard

❦

ONCE upon a time there lived a man who possessed fine
houses in town and in the country, dishes and plates of
silver and gold, furniture all covered in embroidery, and carriages all gilded; but unfortunately the man's beard was blue,
and this made him so ugly and fearsome that all the women and
girls, without exception, would run away from him. Nearby
there lived a noble lady, who had two daughters of the greatest
beauty. The man asked her permission to marry one or other of
them, leaving it to her to decide which daughter she would give
to him. Neither of them wanted him, and each said that the other
one could be his wife, for they could not bring themselves to
marry a man with a blue beard. What put them off even more
was that he had already been married several times, and nobody
knew what had become of the wives.

Bluebeard, in order to get better acquainted, took them and
their mother, with three or four of their best friends, and some
young men who lived in the neighbourhood, to visit one of his
country houses, where they stayed for a whole week. They had
outings all the time, hunting parties, fishing trips, and banquets;
nor did they ever go to sleep, but spent all the night playing
practical jokes on one another; and they enjoyed themselves so
much that the younger of the two sisters began to think that
their host's beard was not as blue as it had been, and that he was
just what a gentleman should be. As soon as they were back in
town, it was settled that they should marry.

After a month had passed, Bluebeard told his wife that he had
to go away for at least six weeks to another part of the country,
on an important business matter. He told her to make sure that
she enjoyed herself properly while he was away, to invite her

friends to stay and to take them out into the country if she wanted to, and not to stint herself wherever she was. 'Here are the keys of the two big store-rooms,' he said, 'the keys for the cupboards with the gold and silver dinner service that is not for every day, and for my strongboxes with my gold and silver coins, and for my jewel-boxes, and here is the master key for all the rooms. As for this small key here, it will unlock the private room at the end of the long gallery in my apartment downstairs.* You may open everything and go everywhere, except for this private room, where I forbid you to go; and I forbid it to you so absolutely that, if you did happen to go into it, there is no knowing what I might do, so angry would I be.' She promised to obey his commands exactly; and he kissed her, got into his carriage, and set off on his journey.

Her neighbours and friends came to visit the new bride without waiting to be invited, so impatient were they to see all the expensive things in the house; they had not dared to come while her husband was there, because of his blue beard, which scared them. And off they went to look at the bedrooms, the sitting-rooms, and the dressing-rooms, each one finer and more luxurious than the one before. Then they went up to the store-rooms,* and words failed them when they saw how many beautiful things there were, tapestries, beds, sofas, armchairs, side-tables, dining-tables, and mirrors so tall that you could see yourself from head to foot, some with frames of glass, some of silver, and some of silver-gilt, which were the most beautiful and splendid that they had ever seen. They kept on saying how lucky their friend was and how much they envied her; she, however, took no pleasure in the sight of all this wealth, because of the impatience that she felt to go and open the door to the private room downstairs.

So keen was her curiosity that, without reflecting how rude it was to leave her guests, she went down by a little secret staircase at the back; and she was in such a hurry that two or three times

*Friends and neighbours envy the new bride's riches*

she nearly broke her neck. When the door of the little room was in front of her she stood looking at it for a while, remembering how her husband had forbidden her to open it, and wondering whether something bad might happen to her if she disobeyed, but the temptation was strong and she could not resist it; so she took the little key and, trembling all over, opened the door. At first she could see nothing, because the shutters were closed. After a few moments, she began to see that the floor was all covered in clotted blood, and that it reflected the bodies of several women, dead, and tied up along the wall (they were the wives whom Bluebeard had married, and whose throats he had cut one after the other). She nearly died of fright, and the key, which she had taken out of the lock, fell out of her hand.

When she had recovered herself a little, she picked up the key again, and locking the door behind her she went upstairs to her room to try to collect her thoughts, but she was unable to, because the shock had been too great. She noticed that the key was stained with blood, and although she cleaned it two or three times the blood would not go away. However much she washed it, and even scoured it with sand and pumice, the blood stayed on it; it was a magic key, and there was no way of cleaning it completely: when the blood was removed from one side, it came back on the other.

Bluebeard returned from his journey that very night, saying that while he was still on his way, he had received letters telling him that the business he had gone to arrange had already been settled to his advantage. His wife did all she could to make him believe that she was delighted at his returning so soon. The next day, he asked for his keys back, and she gave them to him, but her hand was trembling so much that he easily guessed what had happened.

'Why is it', he asked, 'that the key to my private room is not here with the others?'

She replied: 'I must have left it upstairs on my table.'

'Then don't forget to give it to me later,' said Bluebeard.

She made excuses several times, but finally she had to bring him the key. Bluebeard examined it, and said to his wife: 'Why is there blood on this key?'

'I know nothing about it,' said the poor woman, as pale as death.

'You know nothing about it?' said Bluebeard; 'but I do: you have tried to get into my private room. Very well, madam, that is where you will go; and there you will take your place, beside the ladies you have seen.'

She threw herself at her husband's feet, weeping and pleading to be forgiven, and all her actions showed how truly she repented being so disobedient. So beautiful was she, and in such distress, that she would have moved the very rocks to pity; but Bluebeard's heart was harder than rock. 'You must die, madam,' he said, 'this very instant.'

'If I must die,' she said, looking at him with her eyes full of tears, 'give me some time to say my prayers to God.'

'I will give you ten minutes,' said Bluebeard, 'and not a moment longer.'

As soon as she was alone, she called to her sister and said: 'Sister Anne' (for that was her name), 'go up to the top of the tower, I beg you, to see if my brothers are coming, for they promised to come today; and if you can see them, make them a signal to hurry.'

Her sister Anne went to the top of the tower, and the poor woman below cried up to her at every moment: *'What can you see, sister Anne, sister Anne? Is anyone coming this way?'*

And her sister would reply: *'All I can see is the dust in the sun, and the green of the grass all round.'*

Meanwhile, Bluebeard, holding a great cutlass in his hand, shouted as loud as he could to his wife: 'Come down from there at once, or else I'll come and fetch you.'

*The two brothers set upon Bluebeard* ☞

'Please, just a minute longer,' his wife answered, and immediately called out, but quietly: *'What can you see, sister Anne, sister Anne? Is anyone coming this way?'*

And her sister Anne replied: *'All I can see is the dust in the sun, and the green of the grass all round.'*

'Down you come at once,' Bluebeard was shouting, 'or I will fetch you down.'

'I'm coming now,' his wife kept saying; and then she would call: *'What can you see, sister Anne, sister Anne? Is anyone coming this way?'*

And then her sister Anne replied: 'I can see a great cloud of dust, and it is coming towards us.'

'Is that our brothers on their way?'

'Alas! sister, no; it is only a flock of sheep.'

'Do you refuse to come down?' shouted Bluebeard.

'Just a moment more,' his wife answered, and called out: *'What can you see, sister Anne, sister Anne? Is anyone coming this way?'*

'I can see,' she replied, 'two horsemen riding towards us, but they are still a long way off . . . God be praised,' she cried a moment later, 'it's our brothers; I shall wave to them as hard as I can, so that they will hurry.'

Bluebeard began to shout so loudly that the whole house shook. His poor wife came down, and fell at his feet in tears, with her hair all dishevelled. 'That will not save you,' cried Bluebeard; 'you must die.' And taking her hair in one hand, and raising his cutlass in the air with the other, he was on the point of chopping off her head. The poor woman, turning towards him and looking at him with despair in her eyes, begged him to give her a minute or two to prepare herself for death.

'No, no,' he said, 'commend your soul to God,' and raising his arm . . .

At that moment, there was heard such a loud banging at the door that Bluebeard stopped short; the door opened, and at once the two horsemen came in; they drew their swords and ran straight at Bluebeard. He recognized them for his wife's brothers: one was a dragoon guard, the other a musketeer;* immediately he ran to escape, but the two brothers went after him so fast that they caught him before he could get out of the front door. They cut him open with their swords, and left him dead. His poor wife was almost as dead as her husband, without even enough strength to get up and embrace her two brothers.

It turned out that Bluebeard had no heirs, so that his wife became the mistress of all his riches. She used some to marry her sister Anne to a young gentleman who had loved her for years; some she used to buy captains' commissions for her two brothers; and the remainder, to marry herself to a man of true worth, with whom she forgot all about the bad time she had had with Bluebeard.

### THE MORAL OF THIS TALE

Curiosity's all very well in its way,
But satisfy it and you risk much remorse,
Examples of which can be seen every day.
The feminine sex will deny it, of course,
But the pleasure you wanted, once taken, is lost,
And the knowledge you looked for is not worth the cost.

### ANOTHER MORAL

People with sense who use their eyes,
Study the world and know its ways,
Will not take long to realize
That this is a tale of bygone days,
And what it tells is now untrue:
Whether his beard be black or blue,

The modern husband does not ask
His wife to undertake a task
Impossible for her to do,
And even when dissatisfied,
With her he's quiet as a mouse.
It isn't easy to decide
Which is the master in the house.

# Puss in Boots

A MILLER who had three children left nothing for them to inherit, except for the mill, a donkey, and a cat. These bequests did not take long to share out, and neither the solicitor nor the notary* were called in: their fees would soon have eaten up the whole of the miserable inheritance. The eldest son got the mill, the middle one the donkey, and the youngest got only the cat. The young man was inconsolable at being left so meagre a bequest. 'My brothers,' he said, 'will be able to make a decent living if they work together; but as for me, once I've eaten my cat and made his fur into a muff to keep my hands warm, I shall just have to starve to death.'

The cat, who could understand what he said, but pretended not to, said in a calm and serious manner: 'You mustn't be upset, Master; all you need to do is give me a bag, and have a pair of boots made for me to walk among the brambles, and you will see that you are not as badly provided for as you believe.' The cat's master did not expect much to come of this, but he had seen the cat play so many cunning tricks when catching rats and mice,* such as to play dead by hanging upside down by his feet or burying himself in flour, that he had some hope that the cat might help him in his wretched plight. When the cat had been given what he had asked for, he dressed up smartly in his boots and, putting the bag round his neck, he took hold of the tie-strings in his two front paws. Then he set off for a warren where there were plenty of rabbits. In his bag he put bran and sow-thistles,* and then waited, stretching himself out as if he were dead, for some young rabbit, still ignorant of this world's trickery, to come and poke its nose into it in order to eat the food he had put there. Scarcely had he lain down than he got what he wanted: a silly

young rabbit went into the bag, and instantly Master Cat,
pulling the strings tight, caught and killed it without mercy.

Full of pride at his catch, he went to visit the King in his palace, and asked to speak to him. He was shown up to His Majesty's
apartments, where he entered and said, bowing low before the
King: 'Sire, I have here a rabbit from a warren, which My Lord
the Marquis of Carabas' (this was the name which he saw fit to
give his master) 'has commanded me to present to you on his
behalf.'

'Tell your master,' said the King, 'that I thank him, and that
I am well pleased.'

On another occasion, he went into a cornfield and hid himself, holding his bag open again; two partridges went into it, he
pulled the string tight, and caught the pair of them. Then he
went to present them to the King, as he had with the rabbit. The
King was again pleased to accept the two partridges, and tipped
him some money. The cat continued in this way for two or three
months, from time to time taking game from his master's hunt-
ing-grounds to the King.

One day, he found out that the King would be going for a
drive along the river in his coach, with his daughter, the most
beautiful princess in the world, and he said to his master: 'If you
follow my advice, your fortune will be made. All you have to do
is to go bathing in the river, at a place that I will show you, and
then leave everything to me.' The Marquis of Carabas did as his
cat suggested, not knowing what his purpose was. While he was
bathing, the King passed by, and the cat began to shout at the
top of his voice: 'Help! help! My Lord the Marquis of Carabas is
drowning down here!' At his cries, the King put his head to the
window, and recognizing the cat who had so often brought him
game, he ordered his guards to hurry to the rescue of His
Lordship the Marquis of Carabas.

While they were getting the poor Marquis out of the river,
the cat went up to the coach, and told the King that, while his

*Master Cat cries for help to save the Marquis of Carabas from drowning*

master was bathing, some thieves had come and stolen his clothes, even though he had shouted 'Stop thief!' as loud as he could (the cat, the rascal, had hidden them under a large stone). The King at once ordered the Gentlemen of the Royal Wardrobe to go and fetch one of his finest suits for His Lordship the Marquis of Carabas. The King treated him with great kindness, and since the fine clothes which he had just been given added to his good looks (for he was handsome and well-built), the King's daughter found him much to her liking. The Marquis had only to throw a glance at her two or three times with great respect and a little tenderness for her to fall madly in love with him. The King invited him to get into the coach and join them on their outing.

The cat, delighted to see that his plan was beginning to succeed, went on ahead, and having met some labourers with scythes cutting grass in a meadow he said to them: *'Good people mowing the grass: unless you tell the King that His Lordship, the Marquis of Carabas, is the owner of this meadow you are mowing, you will all be chopped up, as fine as sausagemeat.'*

The King did not fail to ask the peasants who owned the meadow they were cutting. 'It belongs to His Lordship the Marquis of Carabas,' they said with one voice, for they were scared by the threat that the cat had made.

'It's a fine estate you have here,' said the King to the Marquis of Carabas. 'Indeed, Sire,' answered the Marquis, 'and that meadow produces an abundant crop every year.'

Master Cat, still going on ahead, met some labourers harvesting, and said to them: *'Good people harvesting the corn: unless you tell the King that His Lordship, the Marquis of Carabas, is the owner of all these cornfields, you will all be chopped up, as fine as sausagemeat.'*

The King came past a moment later, and asked who owned all the cornfields he could see. 'His Lordship the Marquis of Carabas,' replied the harvesters, and the King again congratulated the

*Master Cat orders the labourers to acknowledge the Marquis of Carabas to the King*

Marquis. Master Cat, still going ahead of the coach, said the same thing to everyone he met, and the King was astonished to see how much land was owned by His Lordship the Marquis of Carabas.

Eventually, Master Cat arrived at a fine castle owned by an ogre, who was as rich as could be, because all the lands that the King had passed through were part of the castle estate. The cat, who had taken care to find out who this ogre was, and what he had the power to do, asked to speak to him, saying that he did not like to pass so near his castle without having the honour of paying his respects. The Ogre received him as politely as an ogre is able to, asking him if he would like to rest a while.

'I have been told,' said the cat, 'that you have the gift of turning yourself into all kinds of animals, for instance, that you could change into a lion or an elephant.'

'That's quite true,' replied the Ogre roughly, 'and to prove it, watch me turn into a lion.' The cat was so scared to see a lion standing before him that immediately he sprang up on the roof, which was quite difficult and dangerous because of his boots, which were no good for climbing over tiles. Some time later, seeing that the Ogre had gone back to his original shape, the cat came down, admitting that he had been really frightened. 'I have also been told,' he said, 'but I can scarcely believe it, that you also have the power of taking the shape of tiny little animals, for instance of turning into a rat or a mouse, but I must confess that I think it quite impossible.'

'Impossible?' retorted the Ogre; 'just wait and see'; and in a moment he changed himself into a mouse, which began to run about the floor. No sooner had the cat seen it than he jumped on it and ate it up.

Meanwhile the King had seen the Ogre's fine castle as he went by, and thought that he would like to go inside. The cat, hearing the noise made by the coach as it passed over the drawbridge,

*The Ogre receives Master Cat politely* ☞

ran to meet it, and said to the King: 'Welcome, Your Majesty, to the castle of His Lordship the Marquis of Carabas.'

'My goodness, Marquis!' exclaimed the King, 'is this castle yours as well?—I can't imagine anything finer than this courtyard with all its buildings around it. Let us see what is inside, please.'

The Marquis offered his hand to the young Princess, and following the King, who went first, they entered a great hall, where they found a magnificent banquet. The Ogre had had it set out for his friends, who should have been coming to see him on that very day, but, because they knew the King was there, dared not come in.

The King, delighted by the good qualities of His Lordship the Marquis of Carabas, just like his daughter, who loved him to distraction, said to the Marquis, seeing the great riches that he possessed, and after he had drunk five or six glasses of wine: 'If you want to be my son-in-law, my Lord Marquis, you have only to say the word.' The Marquis bowed deeply, and accepted the honour that the King had done him; and that very day he married the Princess. The cat became a great lord, and never chased a mouse again, except to please himself.

### THE MORAL OF THIS TALE

Although the benefits are great
For one who owns a large estate
Because he is his father's son,
Young men, when all is said and done,
Will find sharp wits and commonsense
Worth more than an inheritance.

## ANOTHER MORAL

If the son of a miller, in ten minutes or less,
Can take a girl's fancy, and make a princess
Look longingly at him, it proves an old truth:
That elegant clothes on a good-looking youth
Can play a distinctly significant part
In winning the love of a feminine heart.

# The Fairies*

❧❧

O NCE upon a time there was a widow who had two daughters.* She and her elder daughter resembled each other so
closely, in appearance and character, that when you saw the
daughter you would have said that it was the mother. They
were both so disagreeable and proud that they were impossible
to live with. The younger of the daughters, who for gentleness
and good manners was the image of her father, was also as beautiful a girl as you could wish to see. Since like attracts like, the
mother was excessively fond of the elder daughter, and had a
terrible aversion for the younger. She made her eat in the kitchen
and work all the time.

Among other things, the poor child was obliged to go a good
half-league from the house twice a day to fetch water, and bring
back a great big ewer filled to the top. One day, when she was at
the spring,* a poor woman came up to her, and asked if she
could have a drink.

'Of course you can, good mother,' said this pretty girl, and
she rinsed out the ewer, went to fill it at the best spot along the
stream, and offered it to the old woman, holding it so that she
could drink more easily. When she had had her drink the good
woman said to her: 'You are so fair of face, so good-natured,
and so considerate, that I cannot do otherwise than give you a
gift' (for she was a fairy, who had put on the shape of a poor
village woman, in order to see how far the young girl's kindness
and politeness would go).

The fairy continued: 'The gift that I give you is this:* at every
word you speak, from your mouth a flower will come, or else a
precious stone.'

*A poor woman asks for something to drink*

When the beautiful daughter arrived home, her mother scolded her for coming back so late from the spring. 'I beg your pardon, mother, for having taken so long,' said the poor girl; and as she spoke, from her mouth came two roses, two pearls, and two great diamonds.

'What's this?' exclaimed her mother in astonishment; 'I do believe that those are pearls and diamonds coming from her mouth; how can that be, daughter?' (which was the first time she had ever called the girl daughter). The poor child told her exactly what had happened, producing huge quantities of diamonds as she did so.

'Really, I must send the other daughter,' said the mother, 'come along, Florrie, look at what has come from your sister's mouth when she speaks. Wouldn't you like to have the same gift? All you have to do is to go and get some water from the spring, and when a poor woman asks for some water to drink, give her some nicely.'

'Not likely,' said the bad-mannered girl, 'that would be a fine sight, me going to that spring.'

'You'll go at once,' said the mother, 'and that's an order.' So she went, but grumbling all the time. She took the finest silver jug that there was in the house. As soon as she had arrived at the spring, she saw a lady, magnificently dressed, approaching from the wood, who came up and asked for a drink. She was the fairy who had appeared to her sister, but she had made herself look and dress like a princess, so as to see how far this daughter's rudeness would go. 'Do you think I've come here just to give you a drink?' said this proud, rude girl. 'I'm supposed to have brought a silver jug on purpose, am I, for Madam to drink from? As far as I'm concerned you can drink straight out of the stream, if you want.'

'That is not very polite,' said the fairy, without getting angry. 'Very well, then; since you are so disobliging, the gift that I give you is this: at every word you say, a toad or a viper will come out of your mouth.'

As soon as her mother saw her, she cried out: 'Well, daughter?'

'Well, mother?' replied the rude girl, and spat out two vipers and two toads.

'Oh Heavens!' exclaimed the mother, 'what's happened? This is all because of her sister; I'll see she pays for it.' And she rushed off at once to give her a beating. The poor child ran away and escaped into the forest nearby.

The King's son, who was on his way back from hunting, met her there, and seeing how beautiful she was, he asked her what she was doing all alone, and what had made her cry. 'Alas, sir! it was my mother, who chased me out of the house.' The King's son, seeing five or six pearls and as many diamonds coming from her mouth, asked her to explain how this could be. She told him the whole story. The King's son fell in love with her, and, considering that the gift she had was worth more than any dowry that another girl could have, he took her back to his father's palace, where he married her.

As for her sister, she made herself so hateful that her own mother chased her out of the house, and the wretched girl, after a long time going from place to place without finding anyone to take her in, went off to die at the edge of a wood.

## THE MORAL OF THIS TALE

If you have gold and jewels galore
You'll make a great effect, of course;
But gentle words are worth much more,
And move us with much greater force.

## ANOTHER MORAL

To be polite and kind, and show respect
Is difficult: some effort must be made;
Sooner or later, though, you'll be repaid,
And often in a way you don't expect.

# Cinderella,
# or The Little Slipper Made of Glass*

❦

THERE was once a gentleman who was widowed, and married again. His second wife was the proudest and haughtiest woman who had ever been seen. She had two daughters, and they were just the same; they resembled her in everything. For his part, the husband had a young daughter, who was amazingly sweet-natured and kind, which gifts she got from her mother, who had been the most charming person you could imagine.

No sooner was the wedding over than the stepmother gave free rein to her bad temper. She could not endure the child's good nature, which made her own daughters appear even more detestable. The worst of the household chores were given to her stepdaughter: it was she who washed the dishes and scrubbed the stairs, she who cleaned out the mistress's bedroom, and the bedrooms of the young ladies her daughters. She slept right at the top of the house, in an attic, on a dirty mattress, while her sisters in their bedrooms had parquet flooring, beds of the most fashionable design, and looking-glasses in which they could see themselves from head to foot.* The poor girl put up with it all patiently, not daring to complain to her father, who would have scolded her, because he was completely under the thumb of his wife.

When she had done all her work, she would go to a corner of the fireplace, and sit among the cinders on the hearth, so that she was commonly known, in the household, as Cinderbum. The younger stepsister, though, who was not as rude as the elder one, called her Cinderella. Even in her ragged clothes, she looked a hundred times more beautiful than either of her sisters, despite their splendid dresses.

One day it happened that the Prince gave a ball, and he invited everyone who was of good family. Our two fine young ladies were included, because they were very important people in those parts. They felt extremely pleased with themselves, and kept themselves busy choosing dresses and hairstyles to suit them, which meant more trouble for Cinderella: for it was she who ironed her sisters' clothes and pleated their cuffs. They could talk of nothing but what they were going to wear. The elder one said: 'I shall put on my red velvet dress and my English lace.' The younger one said: 'I shall put on the skirt I always wear, but to make up for it I shall have my cape with golden flowers and my diamond hairpin, which is something you won't see every day.'

They sent for the best hairdresser in town, to put their hair into double rows of curls,* and went to the best supplier of beauty spots.* They summoned Cinderella to advise them because she had good taste; the advice she gave was perfect. She even offered to do their hair, which they gladly accepted.

While she was doing it, they said: 'Cinderella, wouldn't you like to go to the ball?'

'For pity, sisters—you are making fun; that kind of thing is not for me.'

'Quite right—how everyone would laugh, to see Cinderbum going to the ball!'

Anyone but Cinderella would have done their hair all askew, but she was good by nature and did it very nicely. They were in such transports of happiness that they ate nothing for almost two days, and more than a dozen laces got broken while they were being laced into their corsets to make their waists look thinner.

At last the happy day arrived; they set off, and Cinderella watched them on their way for as long as she could; seeing them no longer, she began to cry.

Her godmother saw that she was all in tears, and asked what the matter was.

'I wish . . . I wish . . .'; but she was crying so much that she could not finish. Her godmother, who was a fairy, said: 'You wish you could go to the ball—is that it?'

'Alas!—yes,' said Cinderella with a sigh.

'Very well; will you be a good girl?' said her godmother; 'then I shall see that you go.'

She took Cinderella to her room, and said: 'Go into the garden and fetch me a pumpkin.'

Cinderella went at once to pick the best one she could find, and took it to her godmother, but could not guess how the pumpkin would get her to the ball. Her godmother scooped out the inside, and when only the skin was left, she tapped it with her wand, and suddenly the pumpkin was transformed into a beautiful golden coach. Then she went to look in the mousetrap, and found six mice all alive. She told Cinderella to lift the trap-door a tiny bit, and as each of the mice ran out, she touched it with her wand, and the mouse changed instantly into a beautiful horse, which made a fine team of six horses, with prettily dappled mouse-grey coats.

As she was puzzled about what to turn into a coachman, Cinderella said: 'I'll go and see if there is a rat in the rat-trap—then we could make a coachman out of him.'

'That's a good idea,' said her godmother; 'go and see.'

Cinderella brought her the trap; there were three big rats in it. The fairy chose the one with the longest whiskers, and when she touched him he turned into a great fat coachman, with one of the finest moustaches that had ever been seen.

Then she said: 'Go out into the garden, and behind the watering-can you will find six lizards; bring them here.' No sooner had she brought them in than her godmother changed them into six footmen, their uniforms covered in gold braid, and they immediately got up behind the coach and held on, as if they had never done anything else all their lives.

Then the fairy said to Cinderella: 'Well, that is what you need to get you to the ball; aren't you pleased?'

*Cinderella's godmother scoops out the pumpkin*

'Yes I am; but must I go like this, in these horrid clothes?'

Her godmother just touched her with her wand, and her clothes were changed at once into a dress made from cloth of gold and silver, gleaming with jewels. Next she gave her a pair of slippers made of glass, as pretty as could be. When she was all dressed up, Cinderella stepped into her coach. Her godmother told her that she must take care, above all else, not to be out later than midnight, and warned her that if she stayed at the ball even a moment longer, her coach would change back into a pumpkin, her horses into mice, her footmen into lizards, and her dress into dirty old rags. She promised her godmother faithfully that she would leave the ball before midnight, and set off hardly able to contain herself for joy.

When the King's son was told that a great princess whom nobody knew had arrived, he hurried to welcome her. He offered her his hand to help her out of her coach, and took her into the ballroom where all the guests were. A great silence fell; the dancers stopped their dancing, the musicians stopped their music, so eagerly were they gazing at the great beauty of the unknown girl. The only thing that could be heard was a murmur of voices exclaiming: 'How beautiful she is!' Even the King, old though he was, could not stop looking at her, and said quietly to the Queen that it was a long time since he had seen so beautiful and charming a girl. All the women were studying her hair and her dress, so that next day they could look the same themselves, provided they could find cloth sufficiently fine and dressmakers sufficiently skilled.

The King's son saw her to a place of honour; then he asked her to dance. She danced so gracefully that she was admired even more. A splendid supper was brought in, but the young Prince ate nothing, because he was so busy looking at her. She went to sit next to her two sisters, and paid them all sorts of attentions; she gave them a share of the oranges and sweet citrons* that she had been given by the Prince, which surprised them very much, since they did not know who she was. While they were talking, Cinderella heard the clock strike a quarter to midnight: at once she made a deep curtsey to all the guests, and went away as quickly as she could.

As soon as she was back home, Cinderella went to find her godmother, and when she had thanked her, she said that what she really wanted was to go to the ball again, on the next evening, because the Prince had asked her. While she was busy telling her godmother about everything that had happened at the ball, her two sisters knocked on the door. Cinderella went to open it.

'What a long time you have been!' she said, and yawned and stretched herself, rubbing her eyes as if she had only just woken up; all the same, she had not been the slightest bit sleepy since she had last seen them.

'If you had come to the ball,' said one of the sisters, 'you wouldn't have found it boring: a beautiful princess was there, the most beautiful you could ever see; to us she was politeness itself, and she gave us oranges and citrons.' Cinderella was beside herself with joy, and asked what the princess was called; but they told her that nobody knew her name, which had made the King's son very unhappy, and that he would give everything he possessed to know who she was.

Cinderella smiled and said: 'She was very beautiful, then, was she? Goodness, how lucky you are! I wish I could see her. Oh please, Miss Javotte, lend me your yellow dress that you wear for everyday.'

'Surely,' said Miss Javotte, 'you don't expect me to agree to that? Lend my dress to an ugly Cinderbum like you? I'd have to be out of my mind.'

Cinderella was expecting to be refused, and she was glad, because it would have made things very difficult for her if her sister had agreed to lend her the dress.

The next evening the two sisters went to the ball again, and Cinderella also, in a dress that was even more gorgeous than the

*Cinderella is admired at the ball* ⤍

first time. The King's son was always at her side, and paid her compliments all the evening. The young lady herself was far from being bored, and she forgot what her godmother had told her, so that she heard the clock strike the first stroke of midnight when she thought it was not yet eleven o'clock: she got to her feet and ran away as fast as a young deer. The Prince went after her and could not catch her; but one of her glass slippers fell off, and he very carefully picked it up.

Cinderella arrived back home quite out of breath, without her carriage or her footmen, and dressed in her old clothes: nothing remained of all her magnificent things, except for one little slipper, the pair of the one which had fallen off. The guards at the palace gate were asked if they had seen a princess leaving; they said that nobody had been seen leaving except a shabbily dressed girl, who looked more like a peasant than a lady.

When her two sisters came back from the ball, Cinderella asked them if they had enjoyed themselves just as much, and whether the beautiful lady had been there. They said that she had, but that she had run away when midnight struck, and in such haste that she had dropped one of her little glass slippers, which was as pretty as could be; that the Prince had picked it up, that throughout the rest of the ball he had done nothing but look at it, and that he must surely be deeply in love with the beautiful girl to whom it belonged.

They were right in what they said, because a few days later the Prince had an announcement made, to the sound of trumpets, that he would marry the person whose foot the slipper fitted. To start with they tried it on princesses; then on duchesses; and then on all the other ladies of the court, but all to no purpose. They brought it to the two sisters at their house, and they did everything they could to get their feet into the slipper, but they could not do it. Cinderella was watching, and recognizing her slipper she laughed and said: 'Let me see if it fits me!' Her sisters began to giggle and make fun of her. The gentleman who was fitting the slipper looked carefully at Cinderella and, finding her very beautiful, said that she was right to ask, and that his orders were to see that the slipper was tried on every girl there was. He asked Cinderella to sit down, and when he brought the slipper to her foot he saw that it went on as easily as if it had been moulded to fit.

The two sisters were completely amazed, and even more when Cinderella took the other little slipper out of her pocket and put it on. At that moment her godmother arrived, and touching Cinderella's clothes with her wand she made them even more splendid than all her other dresses.

Then the two sisters recognized her for the beauty that they had seen at the ball. They threw themselves at her feet and asked her pardon for all that she had suffered when they had treated her so badly. Cinderella made them get up, embraced them, told them that she forgave them with all her heart, and said that she begged them to love her kindly always. She was taken to the young Prince, dressed as she was in all her fine clothes: he thought that she was more beautiful than ever, and a few days later he married her. Cinderella, who was as good-natured as she was beautiful, arranged for her two sisters to live in the palace, and married them on the same day to two great lords at the Court.

### THE MORAL OF THIS TALE

Though beauty's a treasure that women desire,
For everyone's fond of a pretty young face,
Cinderella had gifts with a value much higher,
As she showed in behaving with charm and with grace.

Some say, when they're asked what this story might mean,
That these were the gifts that her godmother gave;
Cinderella had learned from her how to behave
With such grace and such charm that it made her a queen.

Young ladies in quest of a prince, you'll discover
That in winning and keeping the heart of a lover
These gifts from the fairies are always the best,
And count for much more than the way you are dressed;
For with them you will get what you're after with ease,
But without them whatever you do will displease.

## ANOTHER MORAL

You have a great advantage, I admit,
If you receive from Heaven at your birth
Good breeding, courage, sense, a ready wit,
And other things of comparable worth;
But that is not enough, unless you know
How best to use such precious gifts: you need
A godfather or godmother* to show
What you must do in order to succeed.

*The slipper fits Cinderella's foot perfectly*

# Ricky the Tuft

ONCE upon a time there was a Queen and she gave birth to a son, who was so ugly and so misshapen that it seemed doubtful for a long time that he was of human form. A fairy, who was present at the birth, declared that despite this he would still be attractive, because he would be very intelligent. She added that he would even be able, in virtue of a gift which she had just granted to him, to bestow as much intelligence as he had himself on the person he loved best.

All this was some comfort to the poor Queen, who was deeply unhappy at having brought such an ugly little runt into the world. And it is true that as soon as the child began to talk he said all sorts of clever things, while whatever he did had something so ingenious about it that people were delighted. I forgot to say that he was born with a little tuft of hair on his head, so that he was called Ricky the Tuft, Rickett being the family name.*

About seven or eight years later, the Queen of a neighbouring kingdom gave birth to twin girls. The first of them to come into the world was as fair as a summer's day, and the Queen was overjoyed, so much so that it made people afraid that her excessive happiness might be harmful for her. The fairy who had been present at the birth of Ricky the Tuft was there also, and to moderate the Queen's joy she told her that the little Princess would lack any intelligence, and would be as stupid as she was beautiful. This was very distressing for the Queen; but a few moments later she had much greater cause to be unhappy, for when the second daughter was born she was found to be extremely ugly.

'Do not be upset, ma'am,' said the fairy; 'your daughter will have other talents to make up for it, for she will be so intelligent that it will hardly be noticed that she lacks beauty.'

'God send that it may be so,' replied the Queen; 'but would it not be possible for her sister, who is so beautiful, to be given a little intelligence as well?'

'As far as intelligence is concerned, madam,' said the fairy, 'I can do nothing for her, but as regards beauty I can do everything, and since I will do whatever I can to please you, I shall grant her a gift: she will be able to bestow beauty on any person she may choose.'

As the two princesses grew up, their qualities also increased in perfection, and people everywhere talked of nothing but the elder daughter's beauty and the young one's intelligence. However, their defects also worsened with age. The younger Princess became visibly uglier, and day by day the elder grew more stupid. When she was asked something, either she would fail to reply, or else she would say something silly. Besides, she was so clumsy that she could not even arrange a few vases on the mantelpiece without breaking one, or drink a glass of water without spilling half of it over her clothes.

Even though beauty is a great advantage for a young person, the younger Princess was almost always the favourite whenever they were in company together. At first people would go over to the beautiful Princess to see and admire her, but soon they would turn to the intelligent one, to listen to the many entertaining things she would say; and it was surprising to see how, in less than a quarter of an hour, the elder sister had nobody near her, while everyone was standing round the younger one. The elder, despite her great stupidity, noticed this quite clearly, and would willingly have given up all her beauty in order to have half her sister's intelligence. The Queen, wise though she was, could not prevent herself from reproaching her daughter several times for being so silly, which made the poor Princess almost die of misery.

One day, when she had gone alone to a wood in order to lament her unhappiness, she saw coming towards her a very ugly little

man, most unpleasant to look at, but dressed with great magnificence. It was the young Prince, Ricky the Tuft, who had fallen in
love with one of the portraits of her which were to be found
everywhere, and had left his father's kingdom in order to have the
pleasure of seeing and talking to her. Delighted to encounter her
alone, he greeted her with all the respect and politeness imaginable. When they had exchanged the usual civilities, he said, having observed that she seemed very sad: 'I cannot understand,
madam, why someone as beautiful as you are should be as unhappy
as you appear to be; for, although I am glad to say that I have seen
a multitude of beautiful ladies before now, I must admit that I
have never seen anyone whose beauty even approaches yours.'

'If you say so, Sir,' replied the Princess; and that was all.

'Beauty,' Ricky the Tuft went on, 'is so great a benefit that it
makes up for everything else; and when you possess it, I cannot
see that anything can cause you much unhappiness.'

'I'd rather be as ugly as you are,' said the Princess, 'provided
I was clever, than beautiful and stupid like me.'

'Nothing shows intelligence more clearly, madam, than the
belief that one does not possess it, for it is in the nature of this
quality that the more intelligence you have, the less you believe
you have.'

'I couldn't say, I'm sure,' said the Princess, 'but I know I'm
very stupid, and it makes me so unhappy I could die.'

'If that is the only thing that makes you sad, madam, I can
easily put an end to your sorrow.'

'And how can you do that?' asked the Princess.

'I have the power, madam,' said Ricky the Tuft, 'to give as
much intelligence as anyone can have to the person I love the
most, and since you, madam, are that person, you can choose
whether to have as much intelligence as it is possible to have, on
condition that you agree to marry me.'

The Princess was struck dumb with amazement, and made
no answer.

'I can see that you find my proposal disagreeable,' said Ricky the Tuft, 'which does not surprise me; but I will give you a whole year in which to decide.'

The Princess had so little intelligence, and at the same time desired so strongly to possess more, that she could not imagine that the end of the year would ever arrive; and so she accepted the proposal that had been made to her.

No sooner had she promised Ricky the Tuft that she would marry him, on the same day a year later, than she began to feel quite different from before. She discovered in herself an incredible ability to say whatever she pleased, and to say it in a natural, elegant, and simple manner. At once she began a long conversation about romantic matters with Ricky the Tuft, and she spoke with such brilliance that Ricky came to think that he had given her more, by way of intelligence, than he had kept for himself.

When she returned to the palace, the whole court was baffled by the sudden and extraordinary change in her, for now she made as many amazingly witty and sensible remarks as she had previously made silly ones. You would not believe how delighted everyone was at court. The younger sister was the only one not to be pleased, because she no longer had the advantage of being clever, and appeared in comparison only to be a picture of ugliness.

The King let himself be guided by his elder daughter's opinions, and sometimes even held a Council in her apartments. Once the news of the change in her had become known, all the young princes of kingdoms nearby made efforts to make her fall in love with them, and almost every one asked her to marry him, but she could find no one among them who was clever enough; and although she listened to them all, she would not commit herself to any of them. However, one of the princes who arrived was so powerful and rich, so intelligent, and so handsome, that she could not prevent herself feeling favourably disposed towards him. Her father observed this, and told her that he would leave the choice of a husband to her, and that she had only to say whom she had chosen.

Now the cleverer you are, the harder you find it to make a firm decision on this matter, and when she had thanked her father the Princess asked him for more time to think about it. By chance she went for a walk, so as to reflect more easily on what to do, in the very wood where she had met Ricky the Tuft. While she was walking, deep in thought, she heard muffled sounds coming from beneath her feet, as if a number of people were busily coming and going. She listened more carefully, and heard a man say: 'Bring that pot over here'; another said: 'Give me that saucepan'; and another: 'Put some more wood on the fire'. At the same moment, the earth opened before her, and she saw what looked like a great kitchen, full of cooks, scullions, and all the staff needed to prepare a magnificent banquet. A troop of twenty or thirty cooks with meat for roasting came out, and went off into an avenue among the trees, taking their positions around a very long table where, holding their larding-pins* in their hands and with the tassels on their hats* over their ears, they all began to work, keeping time to the sound of a melodious song.

Astonished at the sight, the Princess asked them whom they worked for. 'For the Prince, Ricky the Tuft, my lady,' said the one who seemed to be in charge; 'it's his wedding-day tomorrow.' The Princess, even more surprised than she had been before, remembered all of a sudden that it was a year to the day that she had promised to marry the Prince, Ricky the Tuft, and she felt as if the ground had given way beneath her. The reason why she had not remembered was that at the time when she had made her promise she had been stupid, but when she acquired her new powers of thought from the Prince she had forgotten all her stupidities. She continued her walk, but had gone only twenty or thirty paces before Ricky the Tuft appeared in front of her, richly dressed and in all his finery, every inch a prince who is about to be married.

*A troop of twenty or thirty cooks passes the Princess*

'As you can see, madam,' he said, 'I have kept my word punctually, and I have no doubt that you are here in order to keep your promise, and make me the happiest of men by giving me your hand in marriage.'

'I must tell you frankly,' replied the Princess, 'that I have not yet reached a decision on the point, and it is my belief that I may never be able to make the decision that you wish.'

'You astonish me, madam,' said Ricky the Tuft.

'I can well believe it,' said the Princess, 'and certainly, if I were dealing with a mere brute, a man without understanding, I should be in a very difficult situation. A princess's word is her bond, he would say, and I am bound to marry him, because of my promise; but since the person I am addressing is the most intelligent man in the world, I am sure that he will listen to reason. You will recall that, when I was stupid, I still could not bring myself to marry you; how can you expect me today, having the intelligence you gave me, which also makes me more critical of other people than I was before, to take a decision which I was unable to take previously? If you really meant to marry me, it was very wrong of you to take away my stupidity and make me see things more clearly than I did once.'

'If a man of no intelligence,' Ricky the Tuft answered, 'would be justified—as you suggested a moment ago—in blaming you for not keeping your word, how can you expect me not to do the same in a matter where my entire happiness is at stake? Is it reasonable that those who are intelligent should be in a worse position than those who are not? How can you make such a claim, you who are yourself so intelligent, and so much wanted to be? But allow me to come to the point. Apart from my ugliness, is there anything about me which you find displeasing? Are you dissatisfied with my station in life, my mind, my temperament, or my behaviour?'

'By no means,' replied the Princess; 'I am attracted by all the things that you have mentioned.'

'If that is the case,' said Ricky the Tuft, 'I shall be happy, since you have the power to make me the handsomest of men.'

'How can that be?' asked the Princess.

'It can be,' replied Ricky the Tuft, 'if you love me enough to want it to be; and to remove your doubts, madam, you should know that the same fairy who, on the day I was born, gave me the power to bestow intelligence on any person I chose, also gave you the power to bestow good looks on any person whom you loved and to whom you wished to grant such a favour.'

'If that is how things stand,' said the Princess, 'I wish with all my heart that you should be the handsomest and most attractive prince in all the world; and as far as it lies in my power to do so, I bestow this gift upon you.'

No sooner had she spoken these words, than Ricky the Tuft appeared to her to be the handsomest, best-looking, most attractive man she had ever seen.

Some people affirm that it was not the fairy's magic which worked this transformation, but love alone. They say that the Princess, having reflected on her lover's perseverance, his discretion, and all his good qualities of soul and mind, no longer noticed the deformity of his body or the ugliness of his face; that his humped back appeared to her to be no more than the posture taken by a proud man who is aware of his importance; and that, though before she had observed him hobbling along most dreadfully, she now perceived only a slight stoop, which she found delightful. They say furthermore that his eyes, which had a squint, seemed to her all the brighter for it, and that these cross-eyes were to her mind a sign of passionate love; and finally that his big red nose seemed to her to have a military and heroic air.

However that may be, the Princess immediately promised to marry him, provided that he obtained the consent of the King her father. The King, having been informed that his daughter had a high opinion of Ricky the Tuft, and knowing besides that he was a wise and intelligent prince, accepted him with pleasure as his son-in-law. On the very next day the wedding took place, as Ricky the Tuft had foreseen, and according to the orders that he had given long before.


### THE MORAL OF THIS TALE

Now what you've just read in the story above
Is not a mere fancy but true;
The person you love seems clever to you,
And you always see beauty in someone you love.


### ANOTHER MORAL

A woman may from Nature have perfection
Of face and feature, colouring, complexion,
Beauty beyond what artists can express;
Yet, in inspiring love, these gifts do less
Than something that we cannot see, unknown
Excepting to the lover's eye alone.

# Hop o' my Thumb

❧❧

ONCE upon a time there lived a woodcutter and his wife, who had seven children, all of them boys. The eldest was only ten years old, the youngest only seven. You may find it surprising that the woodcutter had so many children in so short a time; but the fact is that his wife was a quick worker, and never produced fewer than two at once.

They were very poor, and the seven children were a great burden, since none of them was old enough to earn his living. What grieved them even more was that their youngest son was very delicate, and hardly ever spoke a word, which they took to show his stupidity, although it was a sign of intelligence. He was very small; when he was born he was hardly bigger than a man's thumb, for which reason Hop o' my Thumb was what he was called. The poor child was the family scapegoat and was always given the blame for everything. Despite this, he was the cleverest of all the brothers, and had the sharpest wits, and though he did not say much, he listened a lot.

There came a year when times were very hard,* and the shortage of food was so severe that the wretched couple resolved to get rid of their children. One night, after the children had gone to bed, while the woodcutter was sitting beside the fire with his wife, he said, with despair gripping his heart: 'As you can see, we no longer have enough food for the children; I cannot bear to see them dying of hunger before my eyes, and I have decided to take them with me into the wood tomorrow and leave them there to get lost, which will be easy enough; for while they are occupied collecting sticks for firewood, all we will have to do is run away without letting them see.'

'Alas!', said the woodcutter's wife, 'how could you take your own children away in order to get rid of them?' However many times her husband told her how poor they were, she could not agree to his plan: she was poor, but she was their mother. Nonetheless, after reflecting on the pain it would cause him to watch them dying of hunger, she did agree, and went to bed in tears.

Hop o' my Thumb had overheard everything they said, because he could tell from his bed that they were discussing family business, and he had quietly got up and hidden under his father's stool, so as to be able to listen without being seen. He went back to bed and stayed awake throughout the rest of the night, thinking of what he would have to do. He rose early and went down to the edge of a stream, where he filled his pockets with little white pebbles, and came back to the house.

They set off, and Hop o' my Thumb kept quiet, saying nothing to his brothers of what he knew. They went into the deepest part of the forest, where none of them could see the others even from ten paces away. The woodcutter began cutting trees, and the children to gather twigs for making bundles of firewood. Their father and mother, seeing them busily at work, gradually went further away, and then suddenly ran off, along a hidden path.

When the children saw that they were alone, they started to cry and shout as loudly as they could. Hop o' my Thumb let them cry, since he was certain that he would be able to find his way back to their house; while they had been walking along the path, he had dropped the little white pebbles he had in his pockets. He told them, therefore: 'Brothers, never fear; our father and mother have left us here, but I will show you the way back to the house; just follow me.' They followed him, and he led them towards the house by the same path that they had taken through the forest. They did not dare go in at once, but pressed themselves against the door to listen to what their parents were saying.

*Hop o' my Thumb leaves a trail of pebbles*

Just at the time when the woodcutter and his wife were returning home, the lord of the manor had sent them ten silver crowns which had been owing to them for a long time, and which they had given up hope of ever seeing again. It saved their lives, for the wretched couple were dying of hunger. The woodcutter sent his wife out straight away to the butcher's, and because it was a long time since they had had anything to eat she bought three times as much meat as she needed for supper for the two of them.

When they had eaten their fill, the woodcutter's wife said: 'Alas! where are our poor children now? All these leftovers would make a good meal for them. And, William, it was you who wanted to get them lost; I told you we would regret it. What will they be doing now in that forest? Alas and alack! perhaps they have already been eaten by the wolves! It is very cruel of you to abandon your children.' The woodcutter eventually grew impatient, as she repeated a score of times that they would regret it and that she had told him so. If she did not hold her tongue, he said, he would give her a beating. Not that he himself was not upset, perhaps even more than his wife, but rather that she gave him no peace, and he resembled many other men in being very fond of women who speak well, while finding those who have always been right very troublesome.

The wife was all in tears, crying: 'Alas! where are my children now, my poor children?' Then once she said it so loudly that the children outside the door heard her, and started to shout all together: 'Here we are! here we are!' She ran quickly to let them in, and said, as she kissed them: 'How happy I am to see you, my dear children! How tired you must be, and how hungry! Peter dear, you're all covered in mud, come and let me clean you up.' This Peter was her eldest son, whom she loved more than any of the others because his hair was reddish, and hers was as well. They all sat down to table, and ate with such an appetite that it did their parents' hearts good to see them, and the children all talked at once almost all the time as they told them how frightened they had been in the forest.

The good people were full of joy to see their children again, and their joy lasted as long as the silver crowns; but when the money ran out, they fell back into their former despair, and resolved to get the children lost once more, and to make sure of it by taking them much further away than the first time. But however much they tried to keep their plan a secret, Hop o' my Thumb still heard them talking about it. He counted on being able to escape in the same way as before; but although he got up early so as to go and collect some little pebbles, he did not succeed, because he found that the door of the house had been double-locked. He could not think what to do, until the wood-cutter's wife gave them each a piece of bread for their breakfast, when it occurred to him that he could use breadcrumbs instead of pebbles, if he dropped them behind him along the paths where they would be going, and he put the bread away in his pocket.

Their father and mother led them into the thickest and darkest part of the forest, and as soon as they reached it they slipped away secretly along a side path, and left the children there. Hop o' my Thumb was not too worried, since he believed that he could easily find his way by following the trail of breadcrumbs that he had dropped wherever they had passed; but he had a nasty surprise when he could not find a single crumb; the birds had come and eaten them all. So the children were very miserable; the further they walked the more they got lost, and the deeper they went into the forest. Night fell, and a great wind began blowing, which frightened them dreadfully. On every side they thought they could hear the noise of wolves howling, and coming closer to eat them. They hardly dared talk to each other or look round. It started to rain heavily, and they got soaked to the skin. At every step they slipped and fell into the mud, so that when they got up they were all dirty, not knowing how to get their hands clean.

Hop o' my Thumb climbed up into a tree to see if he could make anything out. He looked around in every direction and saw a faint light which looked like a candle, but it was a long way off, outside the forest. He came down from the tree, and when he was on the ground he could no longer see anything. This alarmed him, but when he and his brothers had walked for some time towards the light he had seen, he saw it again as they came out from the wood. At last they reached the house where the candle was, but not without many a scare before they got there, because they had often lost sight of it, which happened whenever their path took them into a dip in the ground.

They knocked on the door and the housewife came to open it. She asked what they wanted; Hop o' my Thumb said that they were poor children who had got lost in the forest, and asked her if she would let them sleep there, out of charity. Seeing what fine boys they were the woman started to cry, saying: 'Alas! my poor lads, what have you done by coming here? Didn't you know that this house belongs to an ogre who eats little children?'

'Alas!' answered Hop o' my Thumb, trembling all over, like his brothers, 'what shall we do? The wolves in the forest are bound to eat us tonight, if you will not give us shelter in your house. And in that case we would prefer the gentleman here to eat us; perhaps he will have pity on us if you would be kind enough to ask him.'

The Ogre's wife, thinking that she could keep them hidden from her husband until the next morning, let them come in, and took them to get warm in front of a blazing fire; for there was a whole sheep roasting on the spit for the Ogre's supper. As they were beginning to get warm, they heard someone knocking loudly on the door three or four times; it was the Ogre coming back. His wife immediately hid them under the bed, and went to open the door. The first thing the Ogre did was to ask whether his supper was ready and whether his wine had been drawn for

*The Ogre demands to know if his supper is ready*

him; then he at once sat down to table. The sheep was still red
with blood, but to him it seemed all the better for it. He sniffed
to right and left, saying that he could smell fresh meat. 'It must
be that calf which I have dressed ready for cutting up that you
can smell,' said his wife.

'I can smell fresh meat, as I've told you already,' retorted the
Ogre, looking crossly at his wife, 'and there's something going
on here that I don't know about.' And as he spoke he got up
from the table and went straight over to the bed. 'Aha!' he said,
'so you have been playing tricks on me, have you! A curse on
you, woman! I don't know why I don't eat you too; it's lucky
for you that you're old and tough. But here's some game that
will do nicely for three of my Ogre friends who should be
coming to see me some day soon.'

He pulled them out from under the bed one after the other.
The poor children knelt down and begged for mercy, but the
Ogre they had to deal with was the cruellest ogre of all, and far
from taking pity on them he was already devouring them with
his eyes, telling his wife that they would be tasty morsels when
she had made a good sauce to go with them. He went to fetch a
carving knife, and went across to the wretched children, sharp-
ening it as he did so on a long whetstone which he held in his left
hand. He had already taken hold of one of the boys when his
wife said: 'What are you doing, at this hour of the night? Isn't
there time enough tomorrow morning?'

'Quiet,' replied the Ogre, 'the meat will taste better if it hangs
longer.'

'You've already got plenty of meat hanging up,' his wife
answered; 'there's a calf, two sheep, and half a pig!'

'You're right,' said the Ogre; 'give them a good supper, so
that they won't get thin, and put them to bed.' The good woman
was delighted, and brought them some supper, but they were
too frightened to eat anything. As for the Ogre, he went back to
his wine delighted to have such a good treat for his friends, and

*The Ogre pulls the boys out from under the bed*

drank twice as much as usual, which went to his head and made him go off to bed.

The Ogre had seven daughters, who were still children. These little ogresses had very fine complexions, because they ate fresh meat like their father, but they had small eyes, very round and grey, hooked noses, and very big mouths that had long sharp teeth with wide gaps in between. They were not yet really wicked, but showed great promise; already they would bite little children to suck their blood. They had been taken up to bed early, and all seven of them were lying in a wide bed, with golden crowns on their heads. Another bed just as wide was in the same room, and in this one the Ogre's wife put the seven little boys for the night, after which she went to bed next to her husband.

Hop o' my Thumb, who had noticed that the Ogre's daughters had golden crowns on their heads, was afraid that the Ogre would feel remorse for not cutting the boys' throats that same night, so he got up in the middle of the night and, taking the caps that he and his brothers were wearing, he put them very gently on the heads of the Ogre's daughters, first removing their golden crowns, which he put on his own and his brothers' heads, so that the Ogre might mistake them for his daughters, and his daughters for the boys whose throats he meant to cut.

It happened just as he thought; for the Ogre, waking up about midnight, was sorry that he had delayed until next day the business that he could have done the day before. He jumped quickly out of bed and took his carving knife, saying: 'Let's just see how my fine little lads are keeping; we'll get it over and done with this time.' He groped his way up to his daughters' bedroom in the dark and went to the bed where the little boys were; they were all asleep, except for Hop o' my Thumb, who was scared out of his wits when he felt the Ogre's hand on his head, after he had tried the other brothers' heads already. Having felt the golden crowns, the Ogre said to himself: 'My word! I'd have made a fine mess of things there. Obviously I drank too much last night.'

Then he went to his daughters' bed, where he could feel the caps belonging to the little boys. 'Aha! there they are,' he said, 'the fine fellows! let's get to work.' And with these words he set to without hesitation and cut the throats of all his seven daughters. And very pleased with himself for having settled the matter so quickly, he went back to bed beside his wife. As soon as Hop o' my Thumb heard the Ogre snoring, he woke his brothers and told them to get dressed and follow him. They went quietly down to the garden and jumped over the wall. They ran almost all night, trembling all the time, and not knowing where they were going.

When the Ogre woke up, he told his wife: 'Go upstairs and dress those lads from last night.' The Ogress was very surprised by such kindness from her husband, not suspecting that he meant her to get them ready for cutting up;* she thought that he was telling her to put their clothes on. She went upstairs, and was completely taken by surprise to see her seven daughters with their throats cut and bathed in blood. The first thing she did was to faint (which is what almost all women resort to first in such circumstances). The Ogre, fearing that his wife would take too long over the task, went up to help, and was just as amazed as she had been when he saw the dreadful spectacle before him. 'Ah! what have I done?' he cried. 'The little wretches!—I'll soon pay them back for this.' He threw a jugful of water in his wife's face, and when she had recovered her senses he said: 'Give me my seven-league boots so that I can go and catch them.'

He set off to track them down, and when he had run great distances in every direction, he finally came upon the children's trail; they were no more than a stone's throw from their father's house. They could see the Ogre stepping from mountain to mountain; he crossed rivers as easily as if they were tiny streams.

*The Ogre cuts his daughters' throats* ☞

Hop o' my Thumb, seeing a hollow in a rock nearby, made his brothers hide in it, and squeezed in after them, watching all the time to see what had become of the Ogre.

The Ogre, who was very weary after having travelled all that way to no purpose (for seven-league boots are tiring for the person who wears them), decided to have a rest; by chance, he came to sit down on the rock where the boys were hiding. He was so exhausted that he could go no further, and after he had rested for a while he went to sleep, and began to snore so dreadfully that the poor children were just as frightened as when he had had his carving knife in his hand to cut their throats. Hop o' my Thumb was not as frightened, and told his brothers that they must escape quickly and run into their house while the Ogre was fast asleep, and that they were not to worry about him. They did as he suggested and soon reached the house.

Hop o' my Thumb went up to the Ogre and gently pulled his boots off; then he put them on himself. They were very big and very wide, but they were magic boots, and had the power of becoming larger or smaller to suit the legs of whoever put them on, so that they fitted Hop o' my Thumb as closely as if they had been made for him. He went straight back to the Ogre's house, where he found the wife in tears beside her daughters who had had their throats cut.

'Your husband is in great danger,' Hop o' my Thumb told her; 'for he has been captured by a gang of robbers, who have sworn to kill him unless he gives them all his gold and silver. Just when they were holding a knife to his throat, he saw me, and begged me to come and tell you of the danger he is in, and say that you are to give me everything he owns that is of value, and not to keep anything back, because otherwise they will kill him without mercy. The message was so urgent that he told me to take his seven-league boots, as you can see, so as to make haste, and also so that you will not think that I am an impostor.' The good woman was very alarmed and immediately gave him everything she had, for the Ogre was a very good husband to her, even though he ate small children. So Hop o' my Thumb, laden with all the Ogre's wealth, went back to his father's house, where he was welcomed with great rejoicing.

Now there are many people who disagree about this last incident, and who claim that Hop o' my Thumb never stole the Ogre's money, although they admit that he had no scruples about taking his seven-league boots, because all they were ever used for was to chase small children. These people declare that their information comes from a reliable witness, since they have in fact been given food and drink in the woodcutter's house. They affirm that, when Hop o' my Thumb put the Ogre's boots on, he went to the King's court, knowing that they were very anxious there about an army that was two hundred leagues away, and wanted to know the outcome of a battle that had been fought. They say that he went to see the King, and told him that if he wished he would bring him news of the army before the day was out. The King promised him a large sum of money if he was successful. Hop o' my Thumb brought the news that very evening, and having made himself well known by this first commission, he was able to earn as much as he wanted, for the King paid him handsomely to carry his commands to the army, and innumerable ladies gave him whatever he wanted in order to get news of their lovers, which brought him more money than anything else. There were some women who entrusted him with letters for their husbands, but they paid him so badly, and it amounted to so little, that he never bothered to count what he had earned in this way.

After he had been in business as a courier for a time, and had amassed great wealth, he went back home to his father's house, where the rapturous welcome he received is beyond all imagining. He gave all his family enough for them to live in comfort, and established his father and brothers in official posts that had just been created;* in this way he started them all on their careers, while improving his own position at Court in the best possible manner.

### THE MORAL OF THIS TALE

If every son grows strong and tall,
Well-mannered and well-liked by all,
Then parents with large families are pleased;
But when a son is silent, weak, and small,
He's likely to be bullied, mocked, and teased.
But sometimes it's the smallest who does best,
And brings prosperity to all the rest.

# APPENDIX A

## Selected Tales related to Perrault's *Contes*

❧❧❧

WHOLE books have been written on the different versions of single tales (see Select Bibliography, items by Cox, Dundes, etc.). What follows is a very small sample, in the form of summaries, chosen because they are relevant to Perrault's versions, not in order to give a truly representative selection of any given tale. The reasons for inclusion are various: because they are more or less probable sources for Perrault, or vary significantly from his tales, or exemplify literary versions contemporary with his, or illustrate the French tradition for a particular tale.

Where possible I have tried to give not only the bare bones of these splendid stories but convey something of their style, sometimes by quotation. For readers who may be interested in pursuing the topic I give the numbers of the tale-type, as found in the basic reference work on folk-tale, known as Aarne-Thompson-Uther, ATU. This is the latest revision (2004), by Hans-Jörg Uther, of Aarne's *The Types of the Folktale*, first published in 1928. For the tales by the Brothers Grimm included below I have used: Grimm, Jacob, and Wilhelm, *Selected Tales*, trans. Joyce Crick (Oxford, Oxford University Press, 2005) (referred to below as Crick), but give the tales their traditional numbering. For the French tales in my most important source, the marvellous repertoire of French folk-tales known as Delarue/Tenèze, I give the editors' own type-numbers, which sometimes differ very slightly from the ATU numbering. I have mostly used two websites, edited respectively by D. L. Ashliman and Heidi Anne Heiner, for texts from *The 1001 Nights*, Straparola, Basile, and Jacobs. For Mlle Lhéritier, Mlle Bernard, and Mme d'Aulnoy, I have referred to the editions by Raymonde Robert and Nadine Jasmin. For further details on all these, see the Select Bibliography. References for some particular tales are given as required below.

## Griselda

ATU type 887, *Griselda*. I have used the translation of the *Decameron* by G. H. McWilliam (Harmondsworth: Penguin, 1972), from which I take the quotations.

Boccaccio, *Decameron*, Tenth Day, Tenth Story: Gualtieri, the Marquis of Saluzzo, is urged by his subjects to marry, so as to ensure an heir, and they offer to assist in finding a suitable wife. In a speech he agrees to their request but states that he will find his wife for himself. He has been attracted by a village girl and arranges with her father to marry her. Announcing his intention to his subjects, he tells them to honour his wife whoever she may be. He makes arrangements and, with a large escort, goes to fetch the unwitting bride. He asks her whether she will always obey him, try to please him, and never be upset by his words or actions; she promises it all. She is then stripped naked before everyone, reclothed and crowned, and the marriage takes place on the spot. As his wife she behaves perfectly to everyone, earning great respect from his subjects, and complies in every way with Gualtieri's wishes. A daughter is born; 'but shortly thereafter Gualtieri was seized with the strange desire to test Griselda's patience, by subjecting her to constant provocation and making her life unbearable'. He feigns anger, telling her that his subjects are discontented with her as a mother because of her previous humble status; she responds with docility. Soon after he sends a man to remove the daughter, apparently to have her put to death. Despite her grief she submits without protest. The child is sent to a relative of Gualtieri's. Similar events occur with the birth of a son, Gualtieri now claiming that the people complain even more because a peasant's grandson will be their lord. Griselda remains outwardly unmoved (although she has been seen 'doting upon the children') when the son also is taken. Years later Gualtieri decides, in a final test, to obtain a papal dispensation allowing him to divorce her and remarry; he arranges for forged letters from Rome to arrive. He tells her that because of her social inferiority she must return to her father as she came, and that he will marry a woman of higher status. In a speech, she accepts his decisions and returns the wedding ring, but recalling her nakedness asks, in return for her virginity, that she should leave wearing at least a smock. Gualtieri, though moved almost to tears, sternly agrees, not allowing the pleas of those present to affect him. Her father, unsurprised, has kept her clothes; she keeps house for him as before. Gualtieri makes preparations for another marriage, and sends for Griselda, telling her to get the house ready for the new bride. 'Since Griselda was unable to lay aside her love for Gualtieri as readily as she had dispensed with her good fortune, his words pierced her heart like so many knives.' She herself in peasant's dress sweeps, tidies, and gives instructions for the decoration of the rooms, then on the wedding day welcomes the guests. The children are brought, but the daughter's identity is carefully kept secret; Griselda welcomes her. When asked by Gualtieri to give her opinion, she praises the girl, but begs him 'not to inflict those same wounds on her that you imposed upon her predecessor'. Seeing her accept the situation still without protest, Gualtieri makes a speech, explaining that his intention was to show her and his people what a wife should be, and that the torments he had made her suffer were intended to prove that he would have peace; now he would make amends. 'These are your children . . . and I am your husband, who loves you above all else.' Joyous reunions follow, with celebrations for days. Gualtieri is regarded as wise but Griselda 'the wisest of all' and her ordeal 'harsh and intolerable'. Her father is treated with honour, her daughter married to a gentleman, and she and Gualtieri live happily together. The final comments compare her to an angel and him to a swineherd, praise her constancy, and suggest that she would have been justified in finding another man after she had been driven out.

## Donkey-Skin

ATU type 510B, *Peau d'Asne*; Grimms no. 15 (see below). Straparola's version appears to be a Donkey-Skin tale with motifs from other types, such as the calumniated queen near the end. Perrault's tale is in outline and some stylistic features close to Basile, but Basile's version lacks the demands made for dresses, and when the heroine leaves home she is transformed, not simply disguised; there is nothing about a donkey, except that the animal is mentioned in two passages.

Straparola, *Doralice* (*Piacevole Notte*, vol. i, Tale 4, a long adventure story): The father of Doralice, a prince of Salerno, remains faithful to his dead wife's wish that he should not remarry; her condition was that only if her ring fitted another woman perfectly could Tebaldo marry her. However, by chance the daughter tries the ring on and says to her father that it fits; not long after, he is 'assailed by a strange and diabolical temptation' to take her to wife. Doralice, when she hears 'the evil designs of her wicked father was deeply troubled in her heart', but is afraid of him and says nothing; she consults her old nurse, who, fearing that mere flight will not succeed, devises a trick: Doralice swallows a potion which puts her to sleep, and is hidden in a clothes-chest, in which she is taken to England. Here she makes her way into a prince's bedroom, still concealed, and looks after it; she is discovered and marries the Prince. The story thereafter concerns their two children and Tebaldo's cunning and ruthless pursuit of revenge (he murders the children, making it look as if their mother had killed them). Eventually, after ever more extraordinary events, the nurse saves Doralice from a terrible death and the villain meets a fitting and no less terrible end.

Basile, L'Orza ('The She-Bear'), Pentamerone, Day 2, Tale 6: A king's wife dies, making him promise not to remarry; after mourning briefly, he seeks a new wife everywhere, but decides that his wife's conditions are met only by his daughter Preziosa. She rebuffs him immediately and firmly, whereupon he orders her to marry him the same evening. She explains her plight to an old woman, who says: 'When your father comes to you this evening—donkey that he is, wanting to act the stallion—put this piece of wood into your mouth, and you will at once become a she-bear.' This happens, and frightens the King; Preziosa, as advised by the old woman, runs away to the forest, where she is seen by another king's son. The she-bear and the Prince form an attachment. One day he sees her in her human form, falls in love, and becomes ill. His mother agrees to his wish that the bear should be in his room and cook for him, which she does, so well that the Queen understands why he is fond of her and allows him and the bear to kiss. 'While thus engaged, I do not know how it happened, but the piece of wood fell from Preziosa's mouth, and she remained in the Prince's embrace, the most beautiful and ravishing being in the world.' All is explained and the lovers marry; nothing more is said of the father.

There is much humour, as in Perrault, but of a folksy, burlesque kind.

Brothers Grimm, no. 65, *Allerleirauh* ('All Kinds of Fur' or 'Coat o' Skins; Crick, 184), is itself found in several versions, from 1812 until 1857. Very briefly: the condition imposed by the Queen who dies is that any future wife of the King should have hair as golden as hers; envoys he sends to search cannot find such a woman, but when the daughter grows up the King falls in love with her. She like his councillors is horrified. On her own initiative she requests three dresses (like sun, like moon, like stars) and a coat made from the skins of every kind of animal, believing that since he cannot give her such things he will no longer pursue her. But he succeeds, and she runs away, to be found in the forest and taken to a palace kitchen. She does the worst work and is mistreated by the cook (an important character), but makes soups for the King in which she places gifts, including a ring; eventually she appears in her dresses, wins the King's love and marries him.

Delarue/Tenèze ii. 256, conte-type, *La Peau d'Ânon* ('The Little Donkey's Skin'), recorded *c.*1885 in east central France: A prince and his wife have a daughter; the wife dies, making the Prince promise never to marry unless it is a woman like herself. In due course he tells his daughter that he wants to marry her. She consults her godmother, who tells her to consent on condition only that he gives her a spinning-wheel which spins by itself. After a long search he finds one. The same happens when she asks for three dresses, like the stars, the sun, and the moon; and for a cabriolet drawn by four rats. The godmother tells her to leave in this, taking all the gifts with her; she will meet shepherds who will sell her a young donkey and skin it for her to wear, when she must look for any kind of menial work. All this happens, and she is employed as a shepherdess, setting the wheel to spin meanwhile. The son and daughter of the estate where she works go to dances, laughing at her when she asks to go too, but the mother allows her to go, for each of three times, beating her beforehand first with a cloth, then a broom, then a poker, but permitting her on each occasion to stay longer. Each time she wears a different dress and is asked where she comes from, answering first 'the land of the cloth', then of the broom, then of the poker. Back home she is told about the beautiful, unknown girl and is mocked when she replies that the girl was no more beautiful than herself. At the last dance it is the King's son who asks her where she comes from; when she leaves, he follows the light of her dress in the darkness and sees her put on the donkey-skin. He falls in love and insists on having a cake made by the shepherdess. She comes to cook for him. While she does so he plucks at the donkey-skin; she pretends to think it is the cat. She puts her ring into the cake before leaving. Finding it, he announces that he will marry its owner. All others having failed to make it fit, she appears in the donkey-skin. When the ring is seen to fit her the Prince says he will wed her and removes the skin, to show her wearing the sun dress beneath. She writes to tell her father, who comes to the wedding.

## Three Silly Wishes

ATU type 750A, *The Three Wishes*, second form.

Philippe de Vigneulles, untitled story, no. 78 in *Cent nouvelles nouvelles* ('A Hundred New Stories'), c.1505–15; from the edition by Charles H. Livingston (Geneva, 1972), 302–7. This begins with a version of ATU type 1430, The Man and his Wife Build Air Castles: A poor and lazy man has an industrious wife, who gets enough milk one Sunday to make a good lot of cheese. Counting on this, they indulge in wishful thinking about getting rich and powerful, until the man gets so excited by the prospect that he spills the milk. Enraged, the wife throws him out, and on his return, seeking to persuade her that she was also to blame, he tells a story against another wife: a poor and lazy couple (like himself, he says), prayed hard and often to God to make them rich. God, 'seeing that their prayers were not founded in reason', granted them three wishes. Delighted at first, they soon quarrel over which of them should wish first. Fearing to lose her opportunity, the wife makes a wish that her cauldron should have a new leg to replace the broken one. The husband is furious, and 'wishes the leg inside her belly'. With it inside, she will die if it is not removed; the neighbours, hearing her cries, all come in, and tell him that he will be a murderer unless he wishes the leg out again. 'Thus were the three wishes all lost and turned to nothing.' The man decides that the poor are destined always to be poor.

Delarue/Tenèze iv (2). 122; conte-type, *Les Quatre souhaits* ('The Four Wishes'), recorded 1883 in Brittany; told by François Marquet, a cabin-boy, aged 16: A poor couple with one son do not have enough to eat. One day when they are resting after working hard, they meet Jesus, who is sympathetic and gives them an ox, telling them that if they cut off its legs they will have four wishes. They take it home and do as directed, wishing each time 'by the virtue of the leg'; first the wife wishes that her son should be bearded like his father, whereupon he grows a large beard and the leg returns under the ox, 'so perfectly joined that it was as if it had never been cut off'. Horrified by the boy's ugliness the wife wishes it removed; and the second leg returns to the ox. The husband storms at his wife, and wishes that she had an ox's leg stuck to her behind, which happens. With only the last wish remaining, the husband offers to ask for gold and silver, so that he will be able to make a golden cover for the leg. She refuses, and herself wishes that the leg might disappear. The ox is now as it had been, and the final comment is that the couple were neither richer nor poorer than before.

*The Three Wishes*, in Joseph Jacobs, *More English Folk Tales*, New York and London: G. P. Putnam's Sons, s.d., first published 1894: A woodman intending to fell a huge oak is addressed by a fairy who implores him not to. Amazed, he agrees, and she grants him three wishes. When he is at home all thoughts of the wishes have gone, but on being told that he will have to wait for his supper he wishes for 'a good link of black pudding'; it at once comes down the chimney. His wife exclaims in astonishment and he recalls what happened that morning. She tells him he is a fool and wishes that the length of sausage was on his nose. It sticks there and they cannot pull it off. He asks what to do. 'T'isn't so very unsightly', she says, but he makes a wish for it to be removed. The final comment is that although they did not become rich they had good black pudding for supper.

## Sleeping Beauty

ATU type 410, *Sleeping Beauty*; Grimms no. 50, *Dornröschen* ('Briar-Rose', which must be derived from Perrault but ends with the marriage; Crick, 323). Delarue/Tenèze, in their Commentary (ii. 70) on the tale, do not regard the version they give as evidence that Perrault's source was a French oral tradition, believing that he used Basile.

Basile, *Sole, Luna e Talia* ('Sun, Moon, and Talia'), *Pentamerone*, Day V, Tale v: A lord has a daughter, Talia. Astrologers predict that she will be in danger from 'a splinter of flax'; he bans it from his house. One day from the window she sees a woman spinning, tries to do it herself, gets a point of flax under her nail, and falls dead. The body is laid out and left abandoned in the lord's country mansion, sitting on a throne. A king out hunting enters the house following his falcon which has flown in, fails to awaken the girl, but is excited and has intercourse with her. Still unconscious, she bears boy and girl twins, called Sun and Moon, and is attended by fairies. Seeking the breast one day, the babies suck on her finger, drawing out the flax, and she comes back to life. The King returns to her and comes to love her more and more; his wife becomes suspicious. She frightens a servant into revealing the truth, and makes him ask Talia to send the children to the King. The Queen orders them to be killed and cooked, but the cook hides them with his wife and prepares lamb instead, which the Queen serves to the King, constantly repeating to him that he is 'eating of his own'. Eventually, irritated, he goes away, whereupon the Queen sends for Talia. Insulting her and refusing to believe her innocent, she prepares a pyre in which to throw her. Talia asks to undress, screaming as she removes each garment; at the last and loudest scream the King reappears. The Queen reproaches him and tells him that he has eaten the children; she is thrown into the fire, together with the servant. The cook, also threatened with burning, is able to explain in time; father and children are reunited and the cook rewarded.

*The Ninth Captain's Tale* (*The 1001 Nights*): A woman, unable to conceive, prays for a daughter even if she is not proof against the smell of flax; she bears a fair and delicate girl, Sittukhan, with whom a sultan's son falls in love. It makes him ill; an old woman discovers the cause and offers to help. She advises Sittukhan to learn to spin, which, despite her mother's protests, she does, but faints when a piece of flax gets behind her nail. The old woman tells the parents not to bury her but put her on an ivory bed in a pavilion in a river, then tells the sick Prince where she is. Finding her, he takes her hand to kiss it, sees the flax and draws it out; then he stays forty nights before leaving, but returns immediately three times on seeing beautiful things—flowers, carobs, a fountain—which remind him of Sittukhan. At last he bids her farewell for ever, whereupon, grieving, she finds a speaking cornelian ring, which gives her even greater beauty and a palace next to the Prince's. He sees her and again falls in love, without recognizing her; he asks his mother to take her precious gifts, brocade, which Sittukhan has cut up, then emeralds, which she gives to pigeons. She tells the Queen that if her son wishes to marry her he must feign death, be wrapped in a shroud and buried in her garden; this is done, and when he is left in the garden she makes herself known and they live together happily.

Delarue/Tenèze ii. 68, *La Belle endormie* ('The Sleeping Beauty'), recorded in the late nineteenth century in south-western France: A rich but ugly and repellent prince asks to marry a beautiful princess, and a meeting between them is arranged at a fair. She refuses him. A fairy godmother of the Prince casts a sleeping spell on her, and she lies sleeping for over a hundred years in a castle, which falls into ruins. No one dares to enter it until a prince loses his way when hunting; having been given shelter and poor food in a hovel he cuts his way into the castle. She wakes and cannot understand what has happened; they marry and live happily.

## Little Red Riding-Hood

ATU Type 333, *Little Red Riding-Hood*. I summarize the Grimms' version because it has superseded Perrault's *Petit chaperon rouge* as the typical form of the story. The version in Delarue/Tenèze below, and others like it, have attracted much critical attention. The mysterious paths were explicated, with reference to rural customs for girls about the age of puberty, by Yvonne Verdier in an influential article which has often been discussed (for instance in Zipes, *Trials . . . of Little Red Riding Hood*, 5–8; see the Select Bibliography).

Grimms no. 26, *Rottkäppchen* ('Little Redcap'; Crick, 91. She includes the sequel, often omitted): A much-loved little girl is known as Little Redcap from the red velvet cap given to her by her grandmother. Her mother sends her one day with cake and wine as a treat for the grandmother, who is ill, and warns her firmly not to stray. As Little Redcap enters the forest where her grandmother's house is she meets a wolf and, unafraid, explains her errand in detail. The wolf suggests that she should pay more attention to the flowers and birds, and she begins to collect a posy, straying from the path, while he goes straight to the grandmother's house. He pretends to be the girl and is told to come in. He eats the grandmother and gets into her bed dressed in her clothes. Little Redcap eventually enters, finding everything strange, and seeing the 'grandmother' exclaims at his ears, eyes, hands, and mouth, at which the wolf 'took one leap out of the bed and swallowed Little Redcap all up'. Then he falls asleep. Hearing loud snores, a passing huntsman looks in, finds the wolf, and cuts open his stomach, releasing the girl and her grandmother unharmed. Little Redcap then puts stones inside the wolf instead, which causes him to die when he wakes and tries to run off. The huntsman gets the skin, the grandmother recovers with the cake and wine, and Little Redcap reflects that she will never stray again.

At some later date, Little Redcap, on a similar errand, meets another wolf, but is not to be led astray and on arrival tells her grandmother about him. The wolf, pretending to be the little girl, fails to get in, and climbs on to the roof to lie in wait for her. Her grandmother tells her to pour the water from a boiling of sausages into a trough outside, and the smell so tempts the wolf that he slides down the roof, falls, and is drowned.

Delarue/Tenèze i. 373: conte-type from east central France: A mother gives her daughter milk and a bun to take to her grandmother. She meets a werewolf, who tells her to take the needles path, while he takes the pins path; she picks up needles as she goes. The werewolf kills and eats the grandmother but puts some of her flesh and blood on one side. When she enters, he tells her to leave the milk and bun and take the meat and wine which is there; the voice of a cat tells her that she is a filthy girl to eat her grandmother's flesh and blood. The were-wolf tells her to undress and get into bed with him. As she takes off each garment she asks what to do with it and is told to burn it since she will have no need for it. In bed, she exclaims at the wolf's hairiness, claws, ears, and so on, and he replies. When she comes to his mouth and he says 'to eat you', she tells him that she needs to relieve herself. Despite being told to do it in the bed, she insists on going outside; the wolf ties her by a piece of wool, but she attaches it to a cherry-tree and runs off. When the wolf discovers that she has gone he chases her, but she reaches home in time.

## Bluebeard

ATU type 312, *The Maiden-Killer (Bluebeard)*. Delarue subdivides, giving Types 311, 312A, and 312B (Delarue/Tenèze i. 182). The closest to Perrault is 312A; 312B has the framework of a Hansel and Gretel tale. The Brothers Grimm included in their first edition a version (no. 30) very like Perrault's, but no doubt for that reason dropped it later; see Crick, 290, 321.

Delarue/Tenèze i. 182; conte-type 311, *Le Gros Cheval blanc* ('The Great White Horse'), recorded in 1946 in Canada: A great white horse abducts girls from a village. A widow with three daughters is forced by her need for firewood to send them, one by one, to collect wood from the forest, where in turn they are caught by the horse (but each time he has to come nearer to their house). He tells them to clean his house while he is out during the day, giving them keys but forbid-ding them to enter one particular room. The two older sisters, on doing so, see dead girls hanging with their throats cut; scared, each drops the key into the blood, which they cannot remove. The horse on his return demands the key, sees the blood, and kills them. The third daughter, however, having recognized her sisters among the corpses, keeps hold of the key. She replaces their heads, and over two days takes them to the barn and wraps them in straw. The horse, see-ing the key free of blood, agrees to her request to take the packages back to her mother. On the third day the youngest daughter makes a large rag doll and puts it in her place by the butter-churn to deceive the horse. Then she wraps herself in straw and is carried back also. The horse on realizing the deceit stamps on the floor so hard that he breaks through it, and is never seen again.

Conte-type 312A, *Le Père Jacques*, from the Vendée area: Bluebeard has killed six wives, and takes a seventh; he goes away, giving her a key but forbidding her to use it. She does so, and sees the six murdered women hanging in their wedding-dresses. She drops the key, it is stained by blood, and she cannot wash it clean. Searching the other rooms she finds an old man, Father Jacques, kept captive in a tower as a lookout. On hearing what she has done he tells her that she will be killed, and that her husband had put something beneath the feet of the other wives which first made them laugh, but then hurt them. The wife sends her dog to her brothers with a message for help. The husband returns, sees the key, and tells her to put on her wedding clothes before she dies. In her room, she plays for time by saying to his repeated requests that she is putting on first this, then that item of clothing. Meanwhile he sharpens his knife, repeating a bloodthirsty refrain as he does so, and she keeps asking Jacques if her brothers are coming. At the moment when she has to admit that she is ready, they arrive and kill him.

Conte-type 312B, from east central France, recorded in about 1885: Two lost sisters are taken in by a housewife, who gives them food to eat that they do not recognize. Then they are shut in a dark room, and threatened with being cooked when her devil husband returns. He removes the elder sister's clothes one by one, with an accompanying series of questions and answers, while the girl asks her sister each time whether she can see anyone coming: a little woman and a little white man are approaching. This couple, who are the Virgin and Jesus, appear as the devil reaches the child's last garment; he and his wife are thrown into the oven.

A version given in abbreviated form, *Comorre*, 191, recorded in 1853 in Brittany, has many elements from the 312A type, but not the key. Comorre, who has married four times already, marries Tryphina, the daughter of a lord. He goes away, leaving her behind. On his return, finding that she is pregnant, he says he will kill her. She is able to escape with the help of the four dead wives, who give her the instruments of their execution (poison, rope, fire, club). She is pursued and killed, but resuscitated by St Veltas. Comorre dies when his castle falls in ruins. On Comorre or Conmar, a historical figure, and the connection between Bluebeard and Brittany, see Warner, *Beast to Blonde*, 260–2.

## Puss in Boots

ATU type 545, *The Cat Helper*. With this tale it is the earlier Italian writer, Straparola, who is closer to Perrault than Basile. The tale in Delarue/Tenèze illustrates a French tradition which differs considerably from Perrault.

Straparola, *Costantino il Fortunato* ('Lucky Costantino'), *Piacevole Notte*, Night XI, Tale i: Costantino, the third son of a poor woman who dies, is left only the cat; his brothers treat him harshly, refusing to give him any of the food they get. The cat by chance is a fairy, who from compassion tells her master that she can help, and catching a young hare she gives it to the King as a present from her master, whom she describes as good-looking and virtuous. She returns to him with food which she has taken surreptitiously (and which he refuses to offer to his brothers). Costantino having suffered from his privations she takes him to the river, washes his skin, and cures him. She continues to offer presents from him to the King, but getting bored she tells her master that if he will follow her instructions she will make him rich. Taking him to the river near the King's palace she tells him to strip and get in, then cries out that Costantino is drowning. He is rescued by the King's servants. The cat tells him that Costantino was bringing jewels as a present but was attacked and robbed. The King decides to give his daughter in marriage to the goodlooking young man, whom he believes to be rich, but when the time comes for the couple, with their escort, to repair to Costantino's castle he has to ask the cat for help. She goes ahead and on meeting some riders tells them that they will be attacked by an approaching force of mounted men; to avoid trouble they must say that they serve Messer Costantino. The same happens with herdsmen and drovers she meets. All tell the King that they serve Costantino. When the cat arrives at a castle she gives the same instructions to the soldiers on guard there; as it happens the castle's owner was away and had met with a fatal accident, so that

Costantino takes possession without difficulty. In due course, having married the King's daughter, he becomes king himself.

Basile, *Gagliuso*, *Pentamerone*, Day II, Tale iv: Remarks against ingratitude introduce the tale. A poor man from Naples dies, leaving to his elder son a sieve, which he is able to use to make money, and a cat to the younger son, who on bemoaning his fate is told by the cat that she can help him. She catches fish in the bay, and gets birds from the fowlers, and takes them to the King as a present, praising Gagliuso. Eventually the King asks to meet him; next day, the cat explains that his servants have stolen all his clothes; the King sends some in replacement. At the banquet they are given the cat has to cover for Gagliuso's ill-bred remarks. She tells the King that Gagliuso's estates further north are vast enough for him to marry a princess; the King sends a group of officials with her to see; in advance, she tells herdsmen and farmers that if they wish to avoid being attacked by the group approaching, they must say that their animals and farms all belong to Gagliuso. Informed of Gagliuso's apparently endless wealth the King, through the good offices of the cat, arranges for his daughter to marry him. After a month the couple set off north, Gagliuso buying a baron's estate with the dowry he has been given. He promises eternal gratitude to the cat, but she, to test him, pretends to be dead, whereupon Gagliuso expresses no regret but tells his wife to throw the body out of the window. With long and bitter reproaches the cat 'threw her cloak about her, and went her way', disregarding his efforts to pacify her.

Delarue/Tenèze ii. 339, conte-type, *Monsieur Dicton*, recorded 1911 in western France: M. Dicton, a poor man whose 'castle' is a hovel, is helped by Renard the fox, who asks to have his only three chickens, one at a time; in return, he first persuades a flock of pheasants to follow him to the King's palace, on the pretext that their tails will be gilded there; he presents them as a gift from M. Dicton. Next he does the same with a flock of woodcock. The third time Renard takes M. Dicton, now in a bad state from hunger, and they find some deer; deceiving them as before, he takes them to the King, who wishes to thank M. Dicton personally. Before he does so, Renard explains his haggard state by saying that he has been attacked and robbed.

The King is invited to visit M. Dicton's castle, Renard going on ahead and ordering the countryfolk to say that all the land around belongs to M. Dicton. Coming to a castle where a party is in progress, he warns its owners that the King is coming with an army to attack them, and hides them in heaps of straw. The King arrives, the food is devoured, and the fox suggests lighting the straw as a celebration, which rids the countryside of the owners to M. Dicton's benefit.

## The Fairies

ATU type 480, *The Kind and the Unkind Girls*; Grimms no. 24, *Frau Holle* (Crick, 86; more elaborate than the Perrault tale). This type is known traditionally as 'Diamonds and Toads', but more usually now as 'The Kind and Unkind Girls'. It is very common, and often regarded as intrinsically connected with the Cinderella type. I give a sample of the French tradition from Delarue/Tenèze. It seems likely that Perrault knew the tale personally as a separate entity; I give Basile's version which has further episodes, together with that published by Mlle Lhéritier, exactly contemporaneous with Perrault's, but designed to give a somewhat different lesson from his.

Delarue/Tenèze ii. 188, conte-type, *Les Deux Filles, la laide et la jolie* ('The Two Daughters, One Ugly and One Pretty'), recorded 1870–5 in the Lyons area: The mother treats the younger, disagreeable, and lazy daughter well, but mistreats the elder, kindly one, making her work. Going to fetch water, she meets the Virgin, who asks her to delouse her hair and enquires what she finds in it; 'gold crowns', says the girl, and is given a box which she is to open at home. When she does so she becomes beautiful. The other daughter, going on the same errand, is asked to do the same for the Virgin, but says she has found lice and fleas; she is given a box which makes her ugly when she opens it. However, the mother goes on treating them in the same way as before.

Basile, *Le Doie Pizzele* ('The Two Cakes'), *Pentamerone*, Day IV, Tale vii: Two sisters, one good and one bad, each have a daughter who resembles her mother. The good cousin, Marziella, sent to get water from a fountain, asks beforehand for a cake to eat there; she sees a hunchback woman who begs a piece, but she gives her the whole cake, and is rewarded: flowers will fall from her mouth, jewels from her hair, and wherever she walks lilies and roses will grow. The next day her mother takes some of the jewels to a usurer. While she is away her aunt visits and hears what has happened; hastening home she sends her daughter Puccia on the same errand, but on meeting the same old woman Puccia eats the cake in front of her; as punishment she will foam at the mouth, her hair will drop toads, and ferns and thistles will grow as she passes. From here on, the story turns to romance between Marziella and a prince, who having heard about her from her brother, wants to see her, but her aunt tries to drown her and sends Puccia instead, with dire consequences; Marziella and the Prince eventually meet through the kind offices of geese that she has fed.

Mlle Lhéritier, *Les Enchantements de l'éloquence, ou les Effets de la douceur* ('The Enchantments of Eloquence, or The Effects of a Sweet Nature'), in her *Œuvres mêlées*, 1695: Blanche is the daughter of a widowed marquis, a worthy man who loses much money and marries a rich widow. She and her daughter Alix are both coarse; they hate Blanche, and she is made to do menial tasks, which she does well. Alix, well dressed and bejewelled, nonetheless has no suitors. Blanche, who reads novels for consolation, is caught by her stepmother but defended by her father, who speaks at length about the educative value of fiction. The family being in the country for the summer, Blanche is sent to fetch water in a wild area at some distance; she is accidentally hurt by a prince out hunting, and impresses him with her sophisticated conversation. Finding out about the family from villagers, the Prince asks one of his fairy godmothers, Dulcicula, to provide a cure for the girl's injury. She visits the family, and is repelled by Alix's hostility and struck by Blanche's charm; her gifts are that the former will be even worse and the latter even better. Cured, Blanche is sent again for water, meets a fine lady and when asked gives her a drink, with great politeness, and again impresses by her conversation. The lady, another fairy godmother, called Eloquentia Nativa, gives her the gift of jewels that come from her mouth. At home, everyone seizes on them. Her stepmother sends Alix to fetch water, despite her protests. This time Eloquentia is dressed as a peasant girl, and on asking to drink from Alix's jug is sent packing, with abuse, and then threatened with violence; she leaves Alix with the gift of spitting out toads, snakes, spiders, and other unpleasant creatures. When this happens, even her mother is repelled by her. Eloquentia takes Blanche to the Prince, whom she marries; Alix wanders the country, falls into destitution and dies alone.

## Cinderella

ATU type 510A, *Cinderella*; Grimms no. 21, *Aschenputtel* (Crick, 78). From the multitude of versions available, the first and second below, from French and Scottish oral tradition, are versions in which the meeting with the Prince occurs at church; in one it is through the father that Cinderella obtains magic gifts, in the other through the mother. The differences between Basile's version and Perrault's imply that he based his on one he knew personally. See also Mme d'Aulnoy's tale *Finette-Cendron*, summarized below with Hop o' my Thumb tales.

Delarue/Tenèze i. 248; conte-type, *Cendrouse*, recorded in 1892 in Poitou: In a rich family with no mother there are two proud sisters and a third, known as Cendrouse, because she likes to be by the hearth. Her sisters often tease her. When they go out she remains at home. Their father goes away to a fair, and asks them what they would like him to bring back; the elder sisters ask for dresses, the third for a hazelnut. When they have the dresses the two go to Mass in them. Cendrouse, opening the nut, finds in it, besides clothes, a coach with driver and horses. With these she too attends Mass. On their return her sisters tell her of the beautiful young lady who was there, to which she says that the lady was no more beautiful than herself; she is mocked. The same happens on the next Sunday, but this time she drops a slipper ('une pantoufle'); it is picked up by a king's son, who swears that he will marry the woman it fits. Next Sunday, all the women try it on, without success, but when Cendrouse arrives, dressed as usual, the slipper fits her; she and the Prince depart together in the coach from the nutshell.

*Rashin Coatie*: a northern Scottish version first recorded by Andrew Lang; text in Neil Philip, *The Cinderella Story*, 60–2: The daughter of a widower who remarries has been left nothing by her mother except a red calf. The stepmother and her three ugly daughters 'did na like the little lassie because she was bonny', and make her wear a 'rashin coatie' ('a garment made from rush fibres'; Philip, 60). She has to sit in a corner of the kitchen and eat scraps, but the red calf gives her all she asks for. The stepmother has it killed. It tells the weeping Rashin Coatie to pick up its bones and bury them under a grey stone. At Christmas everyone except her goes to church in their best clothes, but she has to stay behind to cook the meal. Not knowing how to, she is given a spell to say by the red calf, together with fine clothes to go to church in; 'she was the grandest and the brawest lady there'. A prince falls in love with her. Back home, she is in her coat with the dinner ready when the others return; told about the fine lady, she asks to go with them next day but is rudely rebuffed. The same things happen next day, with 'brawer claes'; on the third day, the Prince tries to prevent her leaving, 'but she jumped ower their heads and lost one of her beautiful satin slippers'. The Prince announces that he will marry the one whom it fits. When nobody can put it on, the stepmother cuts the heel and toes of one of her daughters and it is forced on. She goes with the Prince to be married, but a bird repeatedly sings a rhyme saying that the slipper does not fit her, but does fit the one 'in the kitchen neuk'. The Prince, suspicious, gets the truth from the stepmother. Before he can try the slipper on Rashin Coatie, she goes to the grey stone and returns dressed more richly than ever; 'and the slipper jumped out of his pocket and on to her foot'.

Basile, *La Gatta Cenerentola* ('The Cat Cinderella'), *Pentamerone*, Day I, Tale vi: A widowed prince has a daughter Zezolla, whose governess treats her with affection, but he gets married again, to 'a wicked jade' who is hostile to her. She frequently confides her sorrows to Carmosina, the governess, saying that she wished she had her as mother. Eventually Carmosina offers to give her advice; she accepts. The suggestion is that she should entice the stepmother to look into a big clothes-chest and kill her by bringing down the lid on her neck. Zezolla carries this out, and later cajoles her father until he marries Carmosina. At the wedding a dove appears and tells Zezolla that if she sends any request to the Dove of the Fairies in Sardinia it will be granted. Carmosina discloses that she has six daughters from a marriage previously concealed, and ensures good treatment for them, while Zezolla is reduced to being a kitchenmaid. Before a journey to Sardinia, the father promises his stepdaughters the gifts that they want; Zezolla asks only to be remembered to the Dove of the Fairies, but warns that if he forgets he will be unable to stir. He does forget, and his ship cannot move from port until the captain has a dream in which he is told of the father's negligence. He goes to the fairies' grotto and is given a kind message and a date-tree for Zezolla, with a hoe, a golden bucket, and a silk cloth to tend it. When she plants it it soon grows tall, and from it comes a fairy, who gives her a spell to recite, through which the tree will provide her with fine clothes. A feast-day comes round and the sisters attend the ball; Zezolla recites the spell and receives a pony, rich garments, and pages to attend her. The young King is entranced, and sends a servant to follow her, but she delays him by throwing down gold coins. Back at home, the sisters tell her what she has missed by not going to the ball. The next day she receives from the date-tree more finery, a coach-and-six, and liveried attendants; the King falls in love. This time she escapes the servant by throwing down jewels. The third time, the spell brings her a golden coach and numerous attendants. As she leaves the ball, the King's servant follows the coach; she tells the coachman to go at full speed and in the rush drops one of her slippers. The servant brings it to the King, who orders every woman to attend a banquet; the slipper fits none of them. When he enquires if all are present, Zezolla's father confesses that he has not brought her because she is 'such a graceless simpleton'. After another banquet next day, the slipper darts on to her foot of its own accord. She is crowned queen, and her stepsisters depart in rage.

## Ricky the Tuft

This is not of folk-tale origin, but would appear to have developed out of some kind of collaboration between Perrault, Mlle Lhéritier, and Mlle Bernard. I summarize the two women authors' tales below, as examples of the more literary treatment of a fairy-tale theme. The ambiguous and uncomfortable ending of Mlle Bernard's tale is considered by Collinet, 291, to anticipate the plot of the main novel, in which the heroine is married against her will. Perrault's version can be related to tales of the Frog-Prince type (ATU type 440; Grimms no. 1), in which a princess has a suitor of some repugnant form whom she eventually finds attractive after all.

Catherine Bernard: *Riquet à la houppe*, in her novel *Inès de Cordoue*, 1696: A prince and princess have a beautiful but stupid daughter called Mama, too stupid to realize it; she meets a hideously ugly man who emerges from the ground and tells her that the reason why she is neglected in gatherings is her lack of intelligence, but that he can make her intelligent by putting a spell on her, on condition that she marries him after a year has passed. She agrees, without understanding what she is agreeing to, and soon becomes clever as well as attractive. She has many suitors, of whom she prefers the handsomest, Arada. But when the year is up Riquet appears, and tells her he is the king of the goblins, living underground; in view of her reluctance, he gives her two days to make her mind up to marry him and stay intelligent. She marries him but cannot reconcile herself to his ugliness. She gets a message to Arada, who joins her, but Riquet finds out. Angry, he revises the spell so that she is clever only for him, during the night. However, she finds a way to keep him asleep and to continue her love-affair. One day, by accident, her ruse is discovered, and Riquet finds the lovers together; this time the spell he casts is that Arada and he should look exactly the same. The story ends at this point with the remark that lovers always become husbands eventually.

Marie-Jeanne Lhéritier: *Ricdin-Ricdon*, an episode in her novel, *La Tour ténébreuse et les jours lumineux* ('The Dark Tower and Days of Light'), 1705, supposedly from an ancient chronicle written by Richard Lionheart: The intricate plot concerns a village girl, Rosanie. She is seen by a prince being bullied by her mother and is taken by him to court to work at spinning; her mother has said, but ironically, that she was good at it. In fact she hates it and, aware of her ignorance in dressing and other courtly skills, cannot endure her new life. In despair, she meets a curious stranger who offers to help. On condition that she will remember the name Ricdin-Ricdon in three months' time, he gives her a magic wand, which enables her to spin with extraordinary speed and to dress elegantly. The Prince, falling in love with her, arouses the hatred of a rejected lover, who plots revenge on him; first with the help of a witch and a magician (later revealed to be Ricdin-Ricdon) he is tempted to leave Rosanie for a beautiful princess and her kingdom; then a wicked ambassador attempts to abduct Rosanie, but after an accident to his carriage and a fight she is rescued by three strangers, their leader turning out to be her Prince; then— after he has seen an apparition in which Ricdin-Ricdon, in fact a devil, boasts of a future triumph in getting a girl into his power—he is attacked by three men but fights them off. Meanwhile his father the King has been told that Rosanie is not what she seems, but of royal blood (in fact the princess whose shape the witch of a previous episode had taken on). Failing to remember the name—which she had not written down because at the time she could not write—she confesses her despair to the Prince, who having heard it when seeing the apparition is able to tell her, and all ends happily for them; on being told his name, Ricdin-Ricdon vanishes, screaming horribly.

On the significance of the tale see Warner, *Beast to Blonde*, 175. As she remarks, it recalls Rumpelstiltskin tales rather than *Ricky*, there being no question of a marriage contract between Ricdin-Ricdon and the heroine.

## Hop o' my Thumb

ATU type 327B, *The Brothers and the Ogre*; Grimms: see below. Perrault's tale, although it begins with the hero seemingly a tiny character like the English Tom Thumb, is never considered as a Tom Thumb story, but always as a version of the Hansel and Gretel type (ATU 327A), the classic form of which is the Grimms' story. Delarue, in his commentary on the type (Delarue/Tenèze, i. 325), notes that the Tom Thumb motif is an unnecessary borrowing from ATU type 700, in which the hero's size is crucial, while in Type 327 it is his cleverness that matters. He also says that no complete versions of the tale (i.e. with a plot ending in the defeat of the ogres) are known to antedate the stories by Perrault and Mme d'Aulnoy; see for instance the first summary below.

Basile, *Pentamerone*, Day 5, Tale 8, *Nennillo and Nennella*, begins like *Hop o' my Thumb*: A widower marries a second wife, who hates his two children and makes him take them twice to a forest in order to lose them, but he leaves them with provisions and, the first time, leaves a trail of ashes by which they can find their way back. The second time, after renewed anger from the wife, he makes a trail of bran, which is eaten by a jackass. On hearing the sounds of a hunt, Nennella runs away and Nennillo climbs into a tree. From here on the story diverges from Perrault's, telling how the girl is caught by a pirate and adopted, later to be swallowed by a magical fish, while the boy is found by a prince and taught to be a carver of meat. They are reunited at a sea-side banquet where he hears his sister's voice calling from inside the fish, and all ends happily except for the stepmother.

Delarue/Tenèze i. 306. Divided into subtypes 327A and 327B, the latter including Perrault's *Le Petit Poucet*. Conte-type for 327B: *Furon-Furette*, collected 1945 from central France: A boy and girl are taken to the forest by their stepmother on purpose to lose them. She makes them think she is still near them by leaving a clog hanging on a tree, which when blown by the wind makes the sound of wood being chopped. Lost, they are taken in by a woman married to a devil; she tries to protect them when her husband returns, but he discovers and prepares an oven in which to cook them. Overhearing his plan, they persuade his children to change places with them in the bedroom and exchange gold rings for ones made of silk taken from a broom, thus tricking the devil into cooking his children. Escaping, they are pur-sued; meeting some washerwomen, they are helped to cross a river when the women spread out sheets for them to walk on. Later the women trick the devil into crossing in the same way but let him drown.

Mme d'Aulnoy, *Finette-Cendron*, a story contained in her novel *Don Gabriel Ponce de Leon*, 1697. It will be apparent that after the sisters escape from the Ogre's castle the plot becomes that of a Cinderella story (or rather Perrault's *Donkey-Skin*, which it resembles more than his *Cinderella*): A king and queen, who have three daughters, lose their kingdom and fall into poverty, to such an extent that the mother decides she must get rid of the daughters, Belle de Nuit, Fleur d'Amour, and Finette-Cendron. She leads them out into the wilderness three times in order to lose them. Finette-Cendron has the help of her god-mother, the fairy Merluche, who gives her a white horse for use when necessary. To lead them on their way back home they have first a thread which extends indefinitely, then gravel. On the third occasion, the two elder sisters having always bullied and insulted Finette-Cendron, Merluche advises her to leave them where they are and go back home alone, but she is too good-natured to do so, and they leave a trail of peas behind when led away from home. The birds take them. Lost and with nothing to eat, they sow an acorn and water it; it soon grows into a tree, from which Finette-Cendron sees a marvellous castle, covered in gold and jewels. When the others, disbelieving her, climb the tree to look, they decide that they must go there, hoping to find princes as husbands, and in the night they take Finette-Cendron's beautiful clothes which had been given her by Merluche. She has to follow them looking like their servant. The castle is owned by a one-eyed ogre, whose ogress wife takes them in, consoling them by undertaking not to eat them as soon as he would have done. When the even more monstrous Ogre comes in there is some conflict between them as his wife wants to keep the girls for herself. Finette-Cendron, as servant, is told to heat the enormous oven, but asked whether it is hot enough persuades the Ogre to look himself, whereupon he gets stuck and is roasted. The sisters suggest that the ogress should make herself beautiful to attract suitors, and they do her hair for her; mean-while Finette-Cendron takes an axe and cuts her head off. The two elder sisters, seeing all the Ogre's wealth, take over the castle and make outings, gorgeously dressed, to balls at the nearby town, leav-ing Finette-Cendron to do the housework. When they are out, she finds as she is sitting in the hearth a golden key hidden in the chimney; it opens a chest full of fine clothes and jewellery. She goes secretly to the same ball as her sisters and is not recognized, but makes a sensa-tion there. Told of the unknown lady by her sisters, she murmurs that she was just the same. Visits to the ball continuing, she leaves later than usual one night, and loses a slipper in the dark. The King's son finds it and becomes ill from love. Eventually he tells his mother that he will marry the one whom the slipper fits. The King announces that all women must come to try it on; many try in vain to make their feet smaller. Finette-Cendron, wanting to go, is insulted and told to water the cabbages, but after her sisters leave she dresses up, and finds Merluche's white horse waiting to take her. On the way they pass her sisters and the horse spatters them with mud; Finette-Cendron tells them that 'Cendrillon' despises them as much as they deserve. When she is taken to the Prince's room, the slipper fits, and she produces its pair; general joy ensues, and more so when she says that she is a princess. It turns out that it was the Prince's parents who dispossessed Finette-Cendron's parents; she agrees to marry him on condition that her parents recover their kingdom. When her sisters appear, she treats them kindly and forgives them. The verse moral reiterates that forgiveness is the best revenge for ingratitude.

Grimms: no. 15, *Hänsel und Gretel* (Crick, 58): The story falls into two parts, like Perrault's. In the first, the parents attempt to get rid of their children in the forest, when Hansel plays the leading role; the second centres on the danger that they will be eaten. The main differences from Perrault's tale are that the villain is a witch who has built an edible house into which she lures children, and that she is outwitted by Gretel, who (like Finette-Cendron) tricks her into entering the oven prepared for roasting the children. They return home with the help of a duck on whose back they ride across a wide stretch of water.

# APPENDIX B

## Early Versions of the last part of *Sleeping Beauty* and of *The Fairies*

❧❧

The early variants are italicized.

### Sleeping Beauty

FROM the moment when the Princess wakes up and talks to the Prince until the end of the tale, the first version published, in the *Mercure galant* of February 1696, differed significantly both from the text of the 1695 manuscript and that published in the 1697 volume of the *Histoires ou Contes*, as follows. The Moral was shorter, omitting the lines which give 'a second lesson'. It has sometimes been affirmed that the passages found only in the *Mercure galant* were the work of Mlle Lhéritier. As with the variants to *The Fairies*, comparison with the final state of the text shows that Perrault was concerned always to simplify and shorten his stories.

Be that as it may, they spent four hours talking to each other and still had not said the half of what they wanted. *'Can it be, beautiful Princess,'* said the Prince, and his eyes as he gazed at her spoke volumes more than his words, *'can it be that I was so favoured by destiny that I was born to serve you? Have those beautiful eyes been opened for me alone, while all the kings of the earth with all their power could not have achieved as much as my love?'*

*'Yes, dear Prince,'* replied the Princess, *'at the sight of you I could feel that we were made for one another. It was you whom I had seen, and talked with, and loved while I was asleep. The Fairy had filled my thoughts with the image of you. I clearly knew that he who was to release me from my enchantment would be as handsome as Love himself, and that he would love me more dearly than himself; and as soon as you appeared I recognized you without difficulty.'*

In the meantime, the whole palace had awakened with the Princess. Everyone was eager to carry on with his work, and since they were not in love, they were all dying of hunger; *it was a long time since they had eaten.* The lady in waiting, famished like the rest of them, grew impatient, and said loudly to the Princess that her meal was served. The Prince helped the Princess to her feet; she was fully dressed and her clothes were magnificent, but he took good care not to tell her that she was dressed like a grandmother in the old days, with a starched high collar; it did not make her any the less beautiful. They went into a hall lined with mirrors, where they had their supper, and were served by the officers of the Princess's household. Violins and oboes played old pieces of music, which were excellent, even though they had not been played for almost a hundred years. After supper, without wasting time, *the First Chaplain* married them in the castle chapel, and the lady in waiting saw them to bed. They slept little, for the Princess had little need of it, and the Prince left her as soon as it was morning in order to go home to the town, since his father would be anxious about him.

The Prince told him that he had got lost in the forest while out hunting, and that he had spent the night in a hovel belonging to a charcoal-burner, who had given him cheese and black bread to eat. The King, who was a good soul, believed what he said, but his mother was not convinced; and observing that he went hunting almost every day, and always had some reason to give as an excuse when he had slept away from home for two or three nights, she became certain that he was carrying on some love-affair. She said to him several times, in the hope of drawing him out, that one should enjoy oneself in life, but he never dared to entrust her with the secret; *although he loved her, she made him afraid, because she came from a family of ogres, and the King had married her only because of her great wealth. It was even whispered at court that she had ogreish tendencies, and that when she saw small children going by she found it almost impossible to prevent herself from attacking them, which is why the Prince was reluctant to say anything.*

*He continued for two years to see his beloved princess secretly, his love increasing all the time. This atmosphere of mystery preserved for him the romance of first love, and marriage with all its delights did not diminish the vivacity of his passion. But when the King his father died, and he was in command,* he made his marriage public, and went in a grand procession to fetch his Queen from her castle. A magnificent reception was held for her in the capital, where she made her entrance into the town.

Some time later, the new King went to war against his neighbour the Emperor Cantalabutto. He left the government of the kingdom in the hands of the Queen his mother, *and asked her to take special care of the young Queen, whom he loved more than ever since she had given him two fine children, a girl who was called Dawn and a boy called Day, because of their great beauty.* The King was to be away at the war for the whole summer, and as soon as he had left, the Queen Mother sent her daughter-in-law and the children to a summer residence she had in the forest, so as to satisfy her horrible desires more easily. She went there herself a few days later, and said one evening to her steward: 'Tomorrow evening for supper, *Master Simon*, I want to eat little Dawn.'

[The 1696 text then continues as in the 1697 volume, except that the steward continues to be called Master Simon and there is no reference to onion and mustard sauce ('la Sauce-Robert'), but the final scene includes a speech from the young queen, omitted in 1697.]

There they were, with the executioners getting ready to throw them into the cauldron, *when the young Queen asked to be allowed at least to lament her fate, and the ogress, wicked though she was, agreed. 'Alas and alack!' cried the poor Princess, 'must I die so young? I know that I have been in the world for some time, but for a hundred years I was asleep, and surely that ought to count? What will you say, what will you do, poor Prince, when you return, and your poor little Day, who is so lovable, and little Dawn, who is so pretty, will not be there to kiss you, and I will not be there either? If I weep, it is your tears that I shed, alas! and over your own fate. Perhaps you will avenge us; and you who obey the orders of an ogress, you wretches, your King will roast you to death over a slow fire.' The ogress, hearing that this speech had gone beyond the limits of a lament, cried out in a transport of fury: 'Executioners, carry out my orders, and throw this chatterbox into the cauldron.' At once they approached the Queen and took hold of her robes, but at that moment* the King, who was not expected so soon, rode into the courtyard.

## The Fairies

The dedication manuscript of 1695 contained many passages which were revised for the 1697 publication. Some are the result of a change Perrault made at the beginning; in the manuscript the tale begins with a widower and his second wife, each with a daughter, not with a widow and two daughters. The Opies (*Classic Fairy Tales*, 100 n.) suggest that Perrault made the revision in order that the situation should be different from that at the beginning of *Cinderella*. Other changes were apparently due to the desire to remove anything deemed unnecessary. The manuscript also lacks the second Moral found in the 1697 text.

*Once upon a time there was a gentleman, the widower of a very sweet-tempered and considerate woman, and having had with her a daughter just like her mother, he married for the second time a very haughty and unpleasant woman, whose daughter was of the same disposition as herself, and as ill-favoured and sulky as the other was pretty and polite. However, this woman only loved her own daughter and mortally hated her husband's; she made her eat in the kitchen and do all the worst and nastiest household work, while the bad-tempered sister had nothing to do all morning except attend to her appearance and, in the afternoon, entertain her visitors and make visits herself. Her poor sister went twice a day to fetch water from a spring which was a good half-a-league distant from the house.*

[Apart from minor revisions, the text remained unchanged until the fairy reappears.]

She was the fairy who had appeared to her sister, but she had made herself look and dress like a princess, so as to see how far this daughter's bad manners would go. *The girl, not thinking that the lady was a fairy, said to her in a grumbling tone: 'Do you think I've come here just to give you a drink? I'm supposed to have brought a silver jug on purpose, am I, for Madam to drink from? As far as I'm concerned you can drink straight out of the stream, if you want.'*

*'You are not very polite, young lady,' said the fairy.*

*'I am what I am,' retorted the bad-mannered girl, 'and it's not your business to tell me off.'*

'*Very well, Miss,*' the fairy replied, *without getting angry, 'since you are so uncivil, the gift that I give you is this (since all should be treated as they deserve): at every word you say, a snake, a frog or a toad will come out of your mouth.*'

*As soon as her mother saw her coming back from the stream, she ran to meet her, to see if she had been as fortunate as her sister, and cried out: 'Well, daughter?'*

'*Well, mother,*' *the badly-behaved girl replied, spitting out two vipers and two toads, 'there wasn't much point in sending me all that way.' And out came more toads and more snakes.*

'Oh Heavens!' exclaimed the mother, 'what's happened? This is all because of her sister; I'll see she pays for it.' And she rushed off at once to give her a beating. The poor child ran away and escaped into the forest nearby.

*There, as she sat weeping at the foot of a tree, the King's son, who had missed his way while hunting, saw her, and finding her very beautiful he asked her why she was in tears and appeared to be in such distress.*

'*Alas! sir,*' *she said, for she did not know that he was the King's son, 'I am a poor wretched girl whose mother has sent her away from home.*' The King's son, seeing five or six pearls and as many diamonds coming from her mouth, *asked her to say how such an unheard-of miracle had come about. She told him the whole story. The King's son, who fell in love with her and thought that her gift was worth more than any other fortune imaginable, took her to the palace of the King his father, where he married her a few days later.*

*As for her rude sister, she became so much hated, and was regarded with such horror because of the nasty creatures which came out of her mouth whenever she spoke, that her own mother could bear her no longer and sent her away in disgrace. For a long time the wretched girl wandered from place to place without finding anyone to take her in, and it is said that she went off to die miserably at the edge of a little wood.*

# EXPLANATORY NOTES

꧁꧂

References below to Collinet and Rouger are to the page-numbers in their editions as given in the Bibliography.

## TALES IN VERSE

### Preface

3 *separately*: this Preface was for the 1695 edition of the verse tales, the first to contain all three, which came out before the prose tales were published.

*with reason alone*: Perrault is still on the defensive against Boileau, his enemy in the Quarrel of the Ancients and the Moderns (see Introduction, p. xi); hence the argument based on examples from antiquity.

*Milesian Tales*: or Milesian Fables, a genre of narrative named after Aristides of Miletus (*c.*100 BC), from a city in Asia Minor, who first compiled a collection of such tales. They had a reputation for eroticism.

*Widow of Ephesus*: this famous story, found in the *Satyricon* of Petronius (first century AD), is the best-known example of a Milesian tale. It had been translated in 1682 by La Fontaine, among others, but in 1695 was topical because it had appeared in 1693 among his last pieces in the twelfth book of the *Fables*. The widow, who initially wishes to sacrifice herself to the memory of her dead husband, changes her mind, which gives rise to Perrault's criticism of the tale's morality. She has vowed to die of starvation, with her maid, at her husband's tomb. Nearby, a soldier is guarding the corpse of a hanged robber, in case his family take it away. The widow and the soldier get into conversation. One thing leads to another, and the soldier, returning to his duties, finds that the corpse has been removed; to save him from the death penalty in his turn, it is replaced by the body of the dead husband.

*Lucian and Apuleius*: the long and much-loved story of Psyche is found in *The Golden Ass* or *Metamorphoses* of Apuleius (b. *c.*AD 123), but not in *The Ass* of Lucian (*c.*AD 120–after 180), although this work is considered to be an example of Milesian fable; a surviving shorter version was attributed to him. Psyche, the youngest of three sisters, is so extraordinarily beautiful that she comes to be worshipped instead of Venus.